//TURBO RACERS//

ESCAPE VELOCITY

BY AUSTIN_ASLAN

HARPER
An Imprint of HarperCollinsPublishers

Turbo Racers: Escape Velocity

Text copyright © 2020 by Temple Hill Publishing LLC

Library of Congress Cataloging-in-Publication Data

Names: Aslan, Austin, author.

Title: Escape velocity / by Austin Aslan.

Description: First edition. | New York, NY : Harper, an imprint of HarperCollinsPublishers, [2020] | Series: Turbo racers ; 2 | Audience: Ages 3-7. | Audience: Grades 4-6. | Summary: Twelve-year-old TURBO racer Mace faces hard choices when a sinister threat menaces not only his sport, but the entire world.

Identifiers: LCCN 2019030700 | ISBN 978-0-06-274107-3 (hardcover)

Subjects: CYAC: Racing--Fiction. | Adventure and adventurers--Fiction. | Science fiction.

Classification: LCC PZ7.A83744 Esc 2020 | DDC [Fic]--dc23

LC record available at https://lccn.loc.gov/2019030700

Typography Joe Merkel

20 21 22 23 24 PC/LSCH 10 9 8 7 6 5 4 3 2 1

❖

First Edition

To Bonnie, ////////////////////////
who opened up the world for me,
from top to bottom,
and instilled in me
a passion for exploring it.
"Sheepy, sheepy," Mom!
I'm truly grateful
for all the adventures.

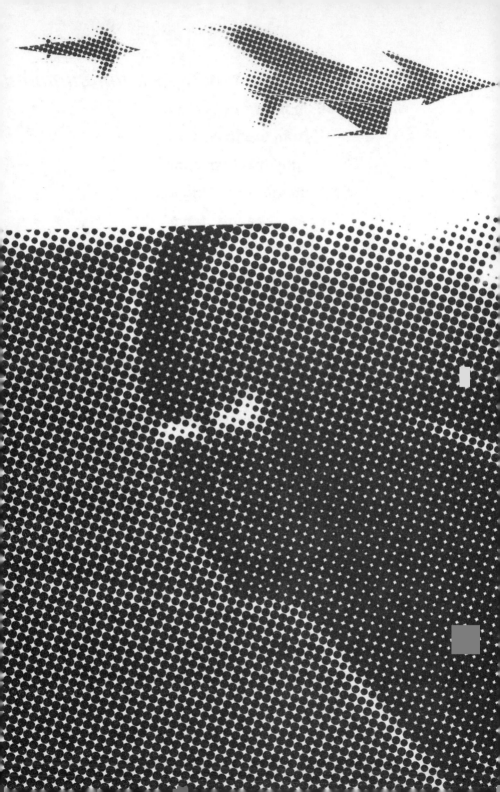

CHAPTER ONE //////

Trailblazer shot out of the Cairo Formula 1 stadium in fourth place, a blue-orange streak ready to morph to air where the road turned to dunes. Mace Blazer gripped the steering wheel, looking for a way to dart past hometown hero Ibrahim al-Aswani. The pilot of gold-red-and-green *Horus* was proving difficult to overtake. And farther ahead of al-Aswani: Darwín Maldonado of *Evolución* and *Lotus*'s Katana.

The final lap through the Egyptian capital city was underway. Mace hadn't dropped below fifth place today. But he hadn't held the lead, either. *Horus* was taking full advantage of its home turf. And Mace had underestimated the tenacity of Maldonado, who had been trading the lead with Katana and eluding Mace all afternoon.

"I'm not worried. Am I worried?" Mace asked his comm.

"You're worried. Just a little," Dex suggested in his ear.

"I am?"

"This'll be over in ten minutes. You're half a mile behind *Evolución*. If you're not making up four and a half feet per second, you won't take the flag."

"Oh, so I should go faster?"

"That might help," Dex replied helpfully. "You might also ask everyone—nicely—if they wouldn't mind slowing down."

"Tried that once," Mace confessed. "Wasn't very effective."

Trailblazer transformed from a roadster into a jet and launched over the dunes into the blue. The air segment was a short hop over a sprawling landscape of tall brick buildings and towering turrets and minarets. Mace mentally mapped out his course over the city bedlam to the ancient Nile, where his morph into the not-so-deep river would require a precise angle, just a smidge steeper than a plane touching down on a runway.

He set his sights on *Horus* and laid into the throttle—but just a little—and climbed past the Egyptian local and into third place. He checked his rear displays. *Guillotine*'s French phenom Leon "Napoleon" Dubois—a distant threat in fifth—was only now rising into the air, cutting left into the helicopter course, where he could engage Katana directly.

Dicers, as they were known, couldn't accelerate as fast as fixed-wing craft, but they could take turns as sharp as bats in a cave. So dicers separated from the pack during air transects, branching onto shorter, curlicue courses and giving audiences a close-up thrill.

Katana was already weaving her dicer, *Lotus*, through a series of canyonesque Cairo streets. Mace had a good view of his rival friend from his higher altitude and noticed her rounding a corner with too much caution. "That's my shot!" Mace cried.

"Finally," Dex agreed, "Aya made *one* mistake."

"That's one more than me." Mace accelerated, feeling the powerful engine behind the cockpit drawing in a greedy breath of air. His own weight against the seat back seemed to double. Blood pooled at his feet; his vision grayed. The smart cushioning squeezed his legs in response, pushing oxygen-rich blood back up into his core, and his eyesight recovered.

And then just as quickly, he decelerated, banking sharply to draw parallel with the river. The negative g's sent his stomach into his mouth. He battled a wave of nausea but maintained control.

It worked. The water entry was flawless—and he dropped below the Nile's surface just ahead of Aya, denying her second place. "Now that's what I call denial!"

"Nope." Dex's voice was dry. "No 'da Nile' jokes on my watch."

"But I waited over two hours to drop that line!"

"My contract specifically stipulates I don't have to hear puns from you."

"You're no pun. You're no pun at all."

"Shut up and finish the job, Mace."

The race flowed against the river's current, which slowed everyone down. Aya began to gain on Mace, and he felt a stab of concern. He needed to keep a healthy margin ahead of her; she'd be a threat later on, no matter what. After all, five races into the season and she'd only bested him in the first matchup, taking silver in Shanghai when he'd taken bronze. She was ravenous for an outright win. But so was Mace. A checkered flag today would put him one race away from securing a berth in his second Gauntlet Prix. Qualifying for the championship race so early in the season would really take the pressure off and keep the Association from breathing down his neck for a while longer.

Technically, Mace was too young to race in the pros. But the league knew if they pulled Renegade from the lineup while he was hot, the fans would lose their minds.

So winning was a matter of survival—it was the only way he could stay in the sport. The fame and the glory and the money were just perks.

Mace would race for free, of course, but he wasn't going to let anyone know that.

He throttled up, and the turbine responded beautifully. "Mace, watch your gauges," warned Dex. "We're getting feedback from the combustor sensor."

I know. That's on purpose. Dex didn't realize that *Trailblazer*'s engine was operating at 100 percent capacity, because Mace had forgotten to tell anyone that he and the trimorpher and a box of tools had had a tinker party last night.

The extra *oomph* he'd engineered was perfectly legal, but risky. The history of racing has forever been a dicey dance between power and panache, after all. Mace hadn't utilized *Trailblazer*'s extra kick yet. But this was the last lap, and he was behind.

Aya inched up on him, slowed, then fell away. Mace exhaled a sigh of relief. He backed off the throttle just enough to stay ahead of her. *Trailblazer* trembled, as if frustrated at backing down, hungry to unleash her full potential. Mace was aware of another racer pushing through the water just behind Aya. Additionally, *Flipside* and *Pendragon* were passing him on the river's surface. Those two were impossible to best on the water, but Mace let his anxiety roll over him. He'd retake the skimmers—the speedboaters—on the other terrains. He always did.

"Your morph's coming up. After an elbow turn. Water-to-ground. Make it matter."

Mace saw the bend, nosed sharply, and punched it for the ramp. His morph to ground was solid, and he took off along the wide-open highway toward the Great Pyramids.

"Okay, Mace," reported Dex, "your engine's wet, and the highway's sandy. It's a cake factory. Remember, avoid the drifts as much as you can, and your morph to air over the pyramids needs to be *steep*. Close your nozzle flaps *before* takeoff. I've reengineered them to filter the sand."

Reengineered them? Mace thought. Dex had been tinkering, too. What if they'd tweaked each other's tweaks? That could spell trouble.

Mace glanced at the roadway. The shoulders were sand dunes. Cairo was a city under constant attack. The whole of it would be buried under feet of sand within years if the residents weren't there to constantly sweep it away. No wonder the ruins of the ancient Egyptians were frequently uncovered, perfectly preserved: the Sahara Desert was a jealous overlord. Time's perfect tomb.

Somehow, Aya had crept back up on him. She drew even, and he caught a glimpse of her glancing at him through her iridescent green-and-purple helmet. She tried to shoot past him, but he pinned her against the highway wall, and she backed off. The next curve was his, and he gleefully pressed his advantage, stealing around her on the inside. He let out a war cry, which quickly turned to a grunt of alarm.

"Napoleon" Dubois came out of nowhere, shooting the gap between Mace and Aya. The next curve in the road was his, and the Frenchman used rival *Pendragon* as a blockade, trapping Mace. Both *Guillotine* and *Lotus* bulleted forward on the inside lane, leaving Mace nosed up, out of momentum, against *Pendragon*'s Arthur MacLeod.

Mace growled his frustration. The air launch was coming up fast. With *Trailblazer*'s flight engine at max capacity, the others would be in for a big surprise.

"Don't forget to toggle the nozzle flaps manually," Dex reminded him.

"Yup." Mace flipped the nozzles, timed his launch, and punched the morph. He took off into the sky, the three pyramids of Giza growing large on the horizon.

He'd lose Aya and Leon now, as they completed figure eights around the pyramids with *Pterodactyl*, *Carpe Diem*, and the other dicers. "Until we meet again," Mace sang to her.

Evolución would be his focus now. They'd go neck and neck on the wider air course. Mace put the Mexican TUR-BOnaut squarely in his sights and throttled all the way, turning to hug the tight bend in the course.

The compressor blades fluttered. *No.* "Dex. You twerked my tweak!"

"I who'd the what?"

The speed. It was too much. Mace's gut lurched. *Think!* His arms jostled, and he lost control of the steering.

The Pyramid of Khufu, the largest of the three great monuments, loomed across his field of view, ballooning. *I'm going to hit!* Mace thought.

Instinct took over. He whipped forcefully to the right. There was an explosion, alarms, gauges flashing—his turbine was on fire, razor-sharp blades spinning off in every direction. They pierced the fuselage. A projectile ricocheted and nicked his leg.

He was in a counterclockwise radial spin, the pyramid tumbling in and out of view. If he smashed against it . . . he'd be instantly dead.

"Turn," he grunted with the effort. "Wide."

"MACE! EJECT!" Dex's voice was wild with terror.

And forfeit? No. "I've got this." His hand, trained to act automatically, fought the g-forces pinning him down. He found the ignition. He shut off the engine. Vented. The fire went out. He slammed the ignition again. The engine sputtered, drew in a breath, came to life! The smart seating clutched him tight. *Trailblazer* shot forward. He steered clear of the pyramid, but . . .

Mace took in his bearings. *Hello, Sphinx.* He adjusted to the left and missed colliding into the mysterious world wonder with half a second to spare.

Goodbye, Sphinx.

Trailblazer was still in one piece.

And Mace was not only still breathing, but still in the running.

"You missed a checkpoint!" said Dex. "Five-second penalty!"

Mace studied his dash. *Yeah, but I'm only three seconds off my previous lap, thanks to where my wild ride ended.* Mace knew this was on account of dumb luck, but no one else had to know that. "I can make it back up. I was going to win by more than five seconds, anyway."

"Well, make your move. The finish is coming up."

Sure enough, the raceway crowded with spectators was just ahead, a giant bowl surrounded by a sea of ancient city. Ibrahim al-Aswani, Aya Nagata, and Darwín Maldonado were all right in front of him where the split air courses converged.

"We're going full throttle," Mace warned.

"Don't risk it. You've already overheated the engine

once. It exploded. Remember?"

Mace glanced at the tear in the thigh of his flight suit, underneath which was a bleeding cut. Had the debris from the explosion entered an inch closer to his femoral artery, it could have killed him. "Oh, yeah. So that's where the hole in my cockpit came from. That's your fault. You unadjusted my adjustments."

"Don't hang this on me," Dex warned. "Stay out of my garage before races. Or at least log your fiddling so I know about it."

Warm desert air hissed in through the breach in the fuselage. Good thing there were no more water entries left in the race. He would have had to call it quits!

"Mace. You're still streaming smoke."

"Again: your fault. But I'll roll with it." Mace throttled to full. He passed the three leaders, dipping under them during their own descent. But he never let off. He needed to win by more than five seconds to make up for the missed checkpoint. That meant he'd have to make his fastest air-to-ground morph *ever*.

The rocket engine exploded again.

Mace was ready this time.

Already going down for a landing, he had his fists locked on the wheel, keeping his flight path razor straight. The new explosion came with an additional boost of speed. *Perfect.* He used it to inch even farther ahead. The unintentional smoke screen would slow his rivals, too.

He dropped his tires at the last possible instant, to reduce drag while still in the air, and he floored the gas before he hit the ground. His wheels grabbed the pavement and yanked him forward, sending him into the arena even faster than when he was flying.

The maneuver cost him control. Landings were always . . . touchy . . . but this one was insane. The speed, the sandy blacktop, the already-spinning wheels. Mace hit the ground, bounced, became a roadster, and lurched forward on the track leading into the raceway.

He was veering toward the stadium wall. Fast.

Don't overcorrect, he thought. Avoiding a spill off the right side of the road only to swerve into the archway bricks would kill him just the same. Mace pressed his hand down on the left side of the steering wheel, as if softly tapping a piano key. The sustained note was just enough. Mace punched through the opening in the stadium wall. He was one with the tarmac, *Trailblazer* carrying him straight and true into the stadium. The grandstands were a blur. The roadway was a streak.

The world was a smear.

Renegade pushed his roadster for all it was worth, entering the long, final quarter turn toward the finish line with no one anywhere near him. But five seconds of lead time at these speeds represented an enormous length of track. Did he have it?

The checkered flag belonged to him. No surprise there. He drove on at top speed. Now the waiting began.

His time? He risked a glace up at the megascreens, saw a live image of *Trailblazer* tightly cutting into the next sharp bank while smoke trailed. The leaderboard was next to the vid. It listed only one team at the moment, an official clock time beside it.

RENEGADE/TRAILBLAZER 2HRS 29MIN
38.092SEC (+5SEC PEN.)

Lotus and *Evolución* entered the raceway together. Mace couldn't determine who was ahead. The next few seconds could have been minutes. And then the leaderboard flickered. Names were added. Times were assigned. Mace locked eyes on the standings.

KATANA/LOTUS . . . . 2HRS 29MIN 43.111SEC (0 PEN.)
MALDONADO/EVOLUCIÓN . . . . 2HRS 29MIN 43.352SEC (0 PEN.)

Mace's mind emptied. He ran a back-of-the-envelope calculation, borrowed the one—and laughed.

By less than two hundredths of a second, Blazer had seized the win.

His racing career remained safe—for now.

CHAPTER TWO //////

Cairo was ancient and bustling—an enormous expanse of brick buildings and hectic roadways. Mace was charmed by the hundreds of mosques and towering minarets. He liked hearing the calls to prayer ring out five times a day from tinny megaphones blasting throughout the city. Even now, the call went out over the Egyptian air.

The balcony of his hotel suite faced the Great Pyramids and the Sphinx. Mace paced ruts into the tiles of the floor as he yo-yoed back and forth between a television broadcasting *TURBOWORLD* in his master bedroom and his balcony view of the world wonders. He liked to absorb the gossip after a race. But the pyramids divided his attention today. The geometric stone monuments—right there, poised at the edge of the city—were mountainous. There was something timeless about them. Bigger than Mace, bigger than TURBO racing. Grander than the moment Mace occupied.

He gazed at the giant stone Sphinx. The stories-tall, half-man, half-lion shrine, crouching partially buried in drifts of sand, won the staring contest.

"No matter what we do, we're just blips in time." It was a strangely comforting thought. It took the pressure off.

"Blip?" a voice in the room challenged. "No, no, no. That's not the right word at all!"

Melanie Vanderhoof was suddenly beside him, gazing out at the pyramids with a different kind of awe. She was Mace's publicist, agent, and personal manager. "You're part of the club," she explained.

"What do you mean?"

Melanie was thirty-three, tall, slender, and had silky blond hair wrapped tightly in a bun. She was dressed in a suit, cradled a large binder in one arm, and adjusted her black-frame glasses with a hand that also held a pen. She stretched out her arm like a circus ringmaster, inviting him to take in their surroundings with new eyes. "Some of the most famous names in history have visited Egypt," she explained. "Mace, you're looking at something Alexander the Great, the emperors of Rome, Cleopatra, the prophet Muhammad, and even Jesus of Nazareth all once gazed upon."

Something tickled awake inside of Mace. That was quite a club she was talking about.

"You're a big deal now. Adjust your thinking," the publicist reminded him. "People will give you the respect you demand. This is a perfect example." She pointed at the Sphinx. "Tell him who you are, Renegade. Go on."

Mace stifled a laugh. But he leaned forward over the balcony anyway, smiling. "I'm Mace Blazer," he tried. It felt silly at first, but there was something undeniably satisfying about it too. He laughed, then impersonated an angry Klingon: "I demand your respect!"

"Exactly. See how that feels?" Melanie prodded.

He rolled his eyes.

"Wait. Were you just barking at the Sphinx?" Dex asked, approaching.

Born in the Dominican Republic, Dex was the same age

as Mace: twelve going on twenty-one. They had been close friends ever since entering the sport together as rivals vying for a chance to secretly pilot a trimorpher sponsored by billionaire inventor Tempest Hollande. Together, along with Aya, they had foiled Tempest's plot to butcher the sport of TURBO by turning it into a no-holds-barred, gladiator-style demolition derby. Mace had won last year's Gauntlet Prix with Dex's help.

Dex could pilot a morpher as well as Mace or Aya. But he was an even better engineer. He'd offered to be Mace's crew chief while saving money to build his own craft. Mace was grateful for the arrangement. There was no one better for the job. And Mace knew—though he'd never say it out loud—that his odds of delivering a repeat Gauntlet victory were far greater with Dex as an ally and not a rival.

"Can we talk?" Dex asked him. "You're blaming me for what happened, but how could I have known?"

Mace gave him a friendly nudge. "It's a simple misunderstanding."

"No, Mace. You could've died. I don't want that on me. Look," he finished, pointing at the living room TV. *Trailblazer*, spewing smoke out its back end as it narrowly missed chopping off more than the Sphinx's already-missing nose, was on constant replay as *TURBOWORLD* commentators Jax Anders and Lee Weisborne offered opinions about Mace's flirtation with disaster.

"He pulled out of it in time, so what's the harm?" Anders was asking.

Weisborne was happy to offer a reply. "The Ministry of Antiquities is having fits. Renegade nearly wiped out a wonder of the world with that stunt. What if he'd rammed it head on?"

"Bug, meet windshield," Mace said with a laugh.

"It's not funny," Dex growled. "Stay in your lane, for once. Cockpit's all yours. Everything under the hood is mine."

Melanie punched the mute button on the remote control. "Fair warning, Mace," she said. "The optics of your near miss are as bad as they look. Your fans love it, of course. But your critics are going for the jugular. The TURBO Association is sending Gimbal herself on our photo-op to the museum. She'd like a word with you."

Mace slouched. "They always want words with me."

"Nothing they can do about you as long as you keep winning," Melanie reminded him.

The distinctive noise of an arriving helicopter echoed from around the corner of the hotel. Melanie's eyes lit up. "That's our ride to Tahrir Square." She snatched her phone and started launching off texts.

Mace straightened, leaving his teacup on the railing. The others followed him inside. He ironed imaginary wrinkles out of his shirt with his hands. "Do I look okay? Spiffy, even?"

"Fit for royalty." Dex sighed.

"Perfect," Mace said. "I'm about to meet a true princess, after all."

Melanie pursed her lips. "Yes, but . . . careful who you say that around. Lots of countries don't recognize the Vaskos' claim to royalty."

"How do *I* look?" Dex asked, checking himself in a large wall mirror. He grabbed his cowboy hat from the table. "Should I wear the hat, or just hold it to my chest?"

"The helicopter will blow it off your head," Mace warned.

"I mean, once we get there."

"You're not coming in the helicopter," Melanie told Dex. "It's too small."

"What?" said Mace and Dex together. "Then you stay behind," Mace told her.

"No, Mace. Sorry," she pushed back. "You and I need to go over protocol for this meet and greet. The wrong kind of handshake and you could ignite a war. Take a cab, Dex."

A knock came at the front door. "That's our cue," Melanie said. "Let's not keep Princess Vasko waiting." She turned and marched out of the hotel room, wrapping a shawl around her head and neck.

Dex grabbed Mace's shoulder and spun him back around. "One more thing. You promised, remember?"

Mace nodded, but he had no idea what Dex was talking about.

"Sponsorship," Dex said firmly.

"Right, right . . . Of course," he said. "I'll put in a good word for you. Cross my heart."

"Okay," Dex said, looking relieved. "Because I need sponsors if I'm going to get behind the wheel of my own racer again." He imagined his personal morpher with a wave of a hand. "*Silverado*. And I can't think of a better sponsor than the Kreznian royal family and Princess Olesya."

"Tempest Hollande?" Mace suggested.

"Har har. If she's even alive, that is."

It was possible Tempest had died in Cuba while escaping

from authorities during last year's Prix. She had fled into an active hypercane, after all. No one had heard a word from her since then as far as Mace knew. Dex squared Mace's shoulders, trying to get his attention.

"Listen," continued Dex. "Since I'm taking a cab to the museum, I should have left an hour ago. With this city's traffic, I'll probably miss the whole event. You have to remember to bring it up? Okay? Don't forget! Promise?"

"I promise." Mace bowed and backed out of the foyer door, letting it shut between him and Dex while making wildly exaggerated royal gestures. "God save the Queen!"

"That's British!" Dex shouted as the door shut.

"Don't you dare say something stupid like that," warned Melanie in the hallway, her face now shadowed by her shawl.

"Okay, I'll say something else stupid."

Melanie ignored him. "Seriously. The situation in Kreznia is very unstable. The royal family's on edge. Watch your step around this girl."

"Then why are we doing this in the first place?"

"You kidding? Mace Blazer and a Kreznian dignitary with Egyptian heritage, strolling among the mummies and swapping cultures while world politicians look on?" She used her

22

hand to flash an imaginary headline. "'TURBO unites the globe!'"

In the elevator, Mace asked her: "Why such a small helicopter? Dex was supposed to join us."

Melanie pushed her glasses up her nose. "This little meet and greet is already feeling like an international summit. Best to keep things simple, Mace. Trust me. I'm your publicist. Like Dex said: stay in your lane. You focus on winning. Let me take care of the rest. Now, about the proper way to greet the princess while we're in Egypt. . . ."

They boarded the waiting helicopter. Mace donned his headset and reached for the seat belt straps but froze. He placed a hand against the ceiling of the cabin, and then added his other palm. Melanie and the pilot watched him, curiously at first, and then impatiently. Mace didn't care. He closed his eyes and continued to feel along the interior surfaces.

"I can't lift off until you're properly secured," the pilot complained over his headset.

Mace opened his eyes, looking pointedly at the pilot. He motioned, cutting his hand across his neck. "Kill it. I'm not flying in this. Something's wrong."

The pilot glowered.

"Just do it," Melanie insisted, already unbuckling herself, worry evident on her features. "He knows what he's doing."

Mace waited nearby for the chopper to grow completely still, then he trotted over to the annoyed pilot and pointed up at the rotor mast. "Look. A linchpin is getting loose on the swash plates. The whole thing could've unraveled at any minute."

"*Ya rrab,*" the pilot exclaimed in a low whisper, with wide eyes and a blanched face. *My god.* He set to refastening the pin so that it was secure. When he was done, he invited Mace to inspect it.

"Looks good," Mace acknowledged. "Let's give it a try."

Everyone piled back in the chopper, and the pilot started it up. Mace took his time feeling out the machine. He could sense a few other minor clicks and a faint rubbing coming from the tail rotor, and explained them to the pilot, but he gave a thumbs-up. "You should inspect those bearings soon, but she'll fly."

They took off, and as they rose, the pyramids and the Sphinx seemed to grow small.

"No curse on you, Mace," Melanie pointed out. "The Sphinx approves. You really are destined for greatness."

Five minutes later, the helicopter touched down on Tahrir Square. Across the plaza was one of the most famous museums in the world—the Museum of Egyptian Antiquities. Mace hopped out of the chopper and involuntarily ducked to avoid the unlikely possibility of being decapitated. He headed for a red carpet lined with reporters and photographers and several dignitaries, mostly men. Mace identified Egyptian politicians he had met before the start of the Cairo Classic. All of them were dressed in traditional bisht cloaks trimmed in gold, and they wore keffiyeh headdresses. There were also some unfamiliar gentlemen decked out in fine suits, probably the Kreznians. In the middle of them all was a pretty girl, wearing neither a traditional hijab nor burqa, but a long-sleeved, dark-blue dress with elegant Arabian designs and plenty of jewelry. She lowered her shawl around her shoulders, revealing a face covered in makeup. She looked younger than Mace had expected.

Princess Olesya Vasko broke from the crowd of dignitaries and walked alone toward him. The cameras behind the rope line flashed like exploding stun grenades. Her eyes locked on his, and she wore a bright, confident smile. "Mace Blazer," she said, holding out a hand for him to shake. "I've

25

been so excited to finally meet you. Congratulations on another impressive win."

Mace had been instructed not to shake her hand in public. He put his own hand to his heart and completed the traditional Kreznian greeting that Melanie had taught him: "Peace be upon you, Miss Vasko."

She laughed and winked at him. "Olesya. Call me Olesya."

The helicopter departed, and a striking silence fell upon Tahrir Square. Mace followed Olesya back to the crowd and shook hands with a number of men in bisht robes and others in tailored suits. He had no idea who any of them were. He thought the formal greetings might never end, but finally the princess led him through a gap in the crowd, and he followed her quickly inside the museum. Melanie eventually caught up to them but stayed several paces back as the Kreznian princess welcomed Mace inside.

Momentarily away from the cameras, she explained, "My mother's father is Egyptian. That's why my connection here is strong even though our royal line rises from the north shores of the Black Coast. When I heard on the news that you've never been to Egypt before, I knew I had found my excuse to corner you." She laughed at her own joke.

Mace felt heat rise into his cheeks, but he tried to play it cool. "Well, thank you for the invitation to show me around. I've always been fascinated by ancient Egypt."

"I see you got a close look at the Sphinx yesterday." Olesya smiled.

Mace nodded along. "I did. I was in a hurry at the time, though. It was all a blur."

Olesya snorted, grew embarrassed, covered her mouth with her hands, then laughed some more.

Mace watched racers Ibrahim al-Aswani and Darwín Maldonado enter the museum lobby. Olesya explained, "I invited the top finishers from yesterday, so there wouldn't be too much speculation about the two of us."

"Speculation?" Mace repeated. "Us?"

Olesya winked. "I invited Katana, also, but she didn't come. Too busy remaining mysterious, I suppose. You know her, correct?" Olesya, with her long black hair, angular face, and warm inquisitiveness, was waiting with genuine interest for an answer.

Mace was having a hard time keeping up. *Did she just wink at me?* "Uh," he said, stalling, letting his mind sort things out. "I don't really know her."

Mace had to choose his words carefully. Olesya was right, of course: Aya was staying away because she couldn't be seen in public without hiding her true identity. She was the same age as Mace, but she hadn't yet revealed that to the world. Her instinct to remain a cryptic—a masked TURBOnaut—had been wise. When Mace had taken off his helmet after he'd won the Glove, he'd created an enormous firestorm of controversy. Safety advocates and child-labor activists and politicians had protested loudly, demanding that underage competitors not be allowed to compete. But TURBO racing had never enjoyed so much press and attention. An enormous fan base had risen up in support of Mace. The Association had backed down, allowing Mace to continue racing for one more season on a trial basis. But other children would not be allowed in the pro league until further review. So Ms. Aya Nagata was stuck as a cryptic.

"Too bad," Olesya said. "I was hoping to discuss the sport with her, from a woman's perspective. Ask my father, he'll tell you: I'm TURBO's biggest fan. Maybe I'll pop behind the wheel of a trimorpher myself."

"You can borrow my keys anytime." It was Mace's turn to wink.

The princess placed a hand on Mace's shoulder. "Thank you. But why would you assume that I don't already have a racer of my own? Hosting—and winning—a TURBO Gauntlet Prix across the Black Coast would be a wonderful way to celebrate my kingdom's independence," she continued. "What a lovely dream. Don't you agree?"

"How old are you?" Mace asked, trying to move out from under her touch.

"Fifteen. I'm old enough to command an army. But I'm not old enough to race." Her look grew playful. "Does that sound fair to you?"

Mace backed up a step. He'd assumed she was older.

He bumped into something and whipped around. Olesya's father—the man who claimed to be king of Kreznia—loomed over him. Beside him was none other than Linda Gimbal, TURBO Association president.

Mace suddenly remembered Melanie's warning: *The TURBO Association is sending Gimbal herself on our photo-op to the museum. She'd like a word with you.*

"Darling." The man in the fine suit spoke to his daughter. "Why don't you greet the other TURBOnauts you invited to join us?"

29

"Yes, father," Olesya said. She gave Mace a mischievous look and pivoted.

"Mace Blazer," the Kreznian began politely, "you've become a wonderful inspiration for us all, especially my free-spirited daughter. I trust you'll enjoy this opportunity to share and learn from each other today. She's used to getting what she wants. But don't get any funny ideas."

"No, Your Highness!" Mace nodded vigorously. "Of course not! I don't have any ideas at all. I mean, I was just . . . I would never—"

"Your Highness?" Olesya's father raised an eyebrow. "Ah. You honor me by recognizing our claim to the Black Coast. But don't think it changes the fact that my daughter is off limits."

Off limits? Mace was floundering on all fronts. "Uh," he tried again. "I'm not—"

Linda Gimbal interrupted mercifully. She was a tall woman with graying Afro-textured hair and stern eyes. "Renegade, perhaps this is an advantageous moment for us to steal away for a second or two?"

Gimbal looked stern. Furious even. But at least she wasn't an offended king. Mace surprised himself, stepping off with her.

CHAPTER THREE //////

Mace and Gimbal huddled against a marble wall. Mace shared a tacit look with Melanie, who watched him closely but made no move to rescue him. *Don't let her bully you!* she mouthed, knowing Mace was an excellent lip reader.

"Stay out of the feud between Kreznia and the rest of the Black Coast," scolded Gimbal. "You're doing enough damage to the sport without taking sides."

"Sorry," Mace said, looking down at his feet. "I don't even know what any of this is about. Why'd you okay the event if everything's so touchy?"

"This was Melanie's idea."

Melanie cleared her throat loudly. Her protest echoed through the museum. Mace glanced up and caught her intense gaze. She pointed over at the camerapeople from the news, who were recording him. *Show your fans you're tough*, she mouthed.

Mace discreetly nodded, but he didn't feel comfortable with where this was going. He looked up at the TURBO president and locked eyes with her.

"You may have bought yourself another race with your checkered flag yesterday. But you almost got yourself killed doing it. Landing at full speed on a blown engine, diving beneath other 'nauts coming in for touchdown—your reckless stunts put everyone at risk. You want to stay in this league, Renegade? Stop piloting like a lunatic and start proving that your wins come from skill, not gimmicks."

The museum lobby had grown quiet. Everyone was watching them. Princess Olesya had come forward, her arms crossed, waiting for his reaction.

Mace gritted his teeth. Words began coming out before his mind could tell him to stop. "You guys can make all the rules you want. I'll obey. I never cheat. But you're fools if you

32

think that'll stop me from winning. I'll always find the weakness. I'll always take advantage of it. That's what a renegade does."

Gimbal watched him, her expression guarded. "When the board meets at year's end to decide if you can continue, we'll be considering a number of factors, not just your star power. And I'll be the one holding the gavel."

"We done here?" Mace stole a glance at Melanie, who pumped her fist. Olesya seemed pleased, too.

Gimbal straightened up, lifting her chin. "This isn't over, Mace, but I can tell when I'm wasting my time with you."

"Great," Mace added, feeling emboldened. "Say hello to your pocketbook for me. Tell it, 'You're welcome.'"

Mace stepped away from Gimbal. His legs felt a little shaky, but it was nothing he couldn't hide. His stomach didn't feel quite right, though; that was harder to ignore.

"Wonderful," Melanie told him in a whisper. "That's going to play well."

"Where's the restroom?" he asked her. She pointed. He made a beeline for privacy, lingering in front of the bathroom sinks for a few minutes to make sure his nerves were calm enough to carry on. He took a few deep breaths, assured himself he wasn't about to spew, and then reemerged into public view.

Princess Olesya returned to Mace. "You respond well to bullies. A trait my father and I admire."

"Um. Thank you," Mace managed, giving her father a wayward glance. He was busy conversing with the Egyptian politicians and wasn't watching the two of them. Mace relaxed a little. "What's the deal with Kreznia, anyway?"

"All shores of the Black Coast rightfully belong to us. We're demanding our land be restored. That's all, really. But I don't want to bore you with that." The princess shrugged him off. "I'm here to learn more about you. The real you—not the TV you. Tell me about your family."

"I'm an only child," Mace answered, thinking the conversation was over.

"What do your parents do for a living?" Olesya asked.

"Oh, um. My mother's a novelist," Mace said. "My father is busy these days starting a new Deaf school in Colorado. Both my parents are deaf."

"You grew up with deaf parents?" Olesya looked amazed. "You can use sign language?"

"I speak American Sign Language, yeah."

"How come I never knew this about you?"

"It doesn't come up much."

"And why should it?" she agreed. "Can I send a donation to your parents' new school?"

"Oh, wow, that'd be great. Thanks!" Mace said. Her generosity jostled loose a memory. There was something on his mind he couldn't shake free. Something he was supposed to ask Olesya. He tried to surface it, but whatever it was, he couldn't summon it up.

She tugged at him, ushering him toward the main hall. "Come on! There's so much to see here. Mummies!"

Huge statues and sarcophagi ringed the perimeter of the central hall. All marble surfaces, the inner . . . *cathedral* of this museum was probably larger than the whole of Mountain Secondary School back home. His amazement must have shown on his face, because Olesya laughed at him over and over as they wandered.

Mace gawked at the exhibits, the repeated busts of countless Roman-numeraled Ramses pharaohs, occasionally trying his best to absorb information about what he was looking at. The hall of mummies held his attention the longest. There was even a room filled with cat and dog and alligator mummies, along with other animals.

Olesya was chatty, happy to share her knowledge of Egyptian mythology with him. He tried asking her more about Kreznia, but she always redirected the conversation. They milled about the popular Tutankhamun exhibit for several minutes. King Tut's riches were extravagant, no doubt about it. As they closely examined the intricate golden helm that had once covered Tut's mummified remains, Olesya commented, "I can't believe he was only a teenager when he died. He had such a fortune, but what was it all worth to him, in the end?"

Mace shrugged. "I don't know. But there's some serious coin in here."

"No, I mean: he still died. He was just a boy."

Mace laughed. "But we're talking about him. Money doesn't buy immortality," he admitted, "but fame sometimes can. And besides, ancient Egyptians believed their wealth followed them into the afterlife."

Olesya frowned. "I'm pretty sure all this treasure is still here on Earth, stuffed into a museum corner."

/////////////////////////

The museum was open to the public, and though Mace and Princess Olesya had a gaggle of handlers and observers in constant orbit around them, they also had time to mingle with average citizens enjoying the exhibits. Which meant lots of requests for selfies. Mace gave his fans what they wanted. He loved seeing how happy it made them. He remembered what it was like to want nothing more than to meet his favorite 'naut.

Olesya paused at a large painting on papyrus and lit up, pointing at a genuinely scary cartoon-like character with hippopotamus feet, lion hands, and the head of a crocodile. "Do you know this story, about Ammit the Devourer?"

"Um, we never covered that freaky goddess at my school. Sorry."

"She's made from the three largest man-eating animals known to Egyptians. She eats your heart in the afterlife if you've been judged a bad person. If your heart weighs more than a feather on the scale, Ammit will swallow your eternal soul."

"That doesn't make any sense," Mace joked. "I know for a fact that my heart weighs about the same as a cantaloupe."

A man came up to them with his phone out, asking for a selfie. The pair granted his request. Then Olesya pulled out her phone and asked the man, "Would you snap one of the two of us, for me?"

Delighted, the museumgoer took Olesya's phone and stepped backward. Olesya put her arm around Mace, and at the last second, she stole a kiss on his cheek as the photo was taken.

Mace pulled back. "Hey. Whoa."

The princess had laughter in her eyes, but also a bit of color in her cheeks.

Olesya's father was suddenly between them, his back to Mace. "Your infatuation with all things TURBO is crossing a line," he declared.

Her expression swirled with devious joy, as if getting her father to rush between them had been her only goal all along. "Father, it's not infatuation, it's research!"

"Save it. Say farewell and then you can apologize to all the guests that you ignored." He pivoted to Mace. "It was delightful meeting you. Have a wonderful day. Good luck with the season."

With that, Olesya was led away. She was able to turn long enough to finger wave at him. "I'll be in touch, Mace Blazer. I'm very curious to see if you can win the Prix this year. It'll be one you never forget."

"Bye," he muttered, on tiptoes to glance one last time at her face as she was enveloped beneath a wall of Egyptian escorts wearing fine linen robes. He sighed. "There goes my shot at living in a castle."

A fan drew near, entering Mace's personal space with more bravado than other photo-seekers. Mace wasn't in the mood for more selfies. "Sorry. Not right now," he said.

"Oh, you don't want my autograph?" asked the person, looking hurt.

"Oh, it's you. How long have you been standing there?" he asked Aya. She was dressed in street clothes and wearing a traditional Egyptian shawl to help her blend in.

"Long enough to be confused," she replied archly. "Your new royal friends didn't set this up because they're your bestie fans, Mace. I hope you realize that."

"Olesya invited you to be here too," Mace told her.

"I know that."

"You should have joined us as Katana."

"Do you know how ridiculous I feel hiding under that helmet? It doesn't work."

Mace remembered quite well how silly it felt to wear a mask in public all the time. "Yeah, that's why I took mine off when I won the Glove."

"I can't wait to do the same thing. But you better watch out, Mace."

"Oh, no, not you, too. I'm hearing it from all sides today."

"I overheard Olesya's father talking to the Egyptians. My Arabic isn't great, but I swear they're up to something. All this TURBO stuff is just a cover."

"No, it's not. The princess wants to become a 'naut. She wants to host a Prix on the Black Coast. That's all."

"This isn't funny, Mace. Remember who you are, or at least who you *were*."

"What's that supposed to mean?"

"You know I respect you. We've been through too much together. But maybe you should check yourself before your crazy new attitude goes off the deep end."

Mace thought of the school he was helping his parents start. He thought of the smiles of the fans who had snapped selfies with him and the princess today. "Thanks, Aya. But you don't need to worry about me. And as long as you keep beating the other dicers and placing all the time, you have nothing to worry about."

Aya wasn't done. "Don't patronize me. If you flame out, you're going to ruin my shot—and you'll kill Dex's chances of racing before he even gets started."

"Dex!" Mace barked, suddenly remembering what had been nagging at him. His stomach sank. "I forgot to ask the Vaskos about sponsoring him."

"Just watch yourself, okay? That's all I'm asking. For everyone's sake," Aya said, her eyes growing soft with concern. "I'll see you in the Alps in two weeks, right?"

"Of course," Mace said as Aya left. "See you at the finish line."

Mace stood alone in front of the enormous display of Ammit the Devourer for a moment, staring at that scary half-crocodile face. But he wasn't worried. He really wasn't. His heart was as light and fluffy as the whipped cream on top of an ice cream sundae. Being a winner wasn't something he needed to apologize for. His fans knew that. Melanie had been drilling that very message home for weeks. Olesya knew it in her bones—she was demanding a whole country be returned to her family! Why couldn't Linda Gimbal and Aya see it, too?

"What'd I miss?"

Mace jumped. He spun around. "Dex! Hey!"

"How'd it go with the princess?" his friend asked. "Why'd you split up?"

Mace let out a dry half chuckle. "Split up. Ha. Date wasn't working out, I guess."

Dex rolled his eyes. "Shut up. Did you at least get a chance to ask her about sponsoring me?"

Mace grimaced. "I'm sorry, Dex. I tried, but, it was never the right moment to bring it up. And then her dad was all, like, 'We're out of here!'"

Dex didn't look mad. Mace could have handled mad. Instead, Dex looked like he was expecting as much. "Thanks a lot, buddy. After all I do for you, you can't even bring the subject up. I'm starting to think that you're holding me back on purpose. You don't want me racing against you. Is that it?"

"No! I swear!" Mace said. "Aya thinks the Vaskos are bad news, and I tend to agree with her, truth be told. There're other sponsors out there."

"Whatever. You mess with my engineering without consulting me. You're not helping me get my own morpher. I'm getting tired of how one-sided our friendship has gotten. Maybe you'd be better off with Carson Gerber as your crew chief."

Carson was Mace's nemesis-turned-good-friend from back home. He and his dad had helped Mace and Dex rebuild *Trailblazer* in time to qualify for last year's Prix. "Dex, don't."

"Enjoy your helicopter ride to the hotel." Dex strode away, shaking his head, his hands in his pockets.

Mace watched his friend turn the corner, and then his gaze drifted once again to Ammit the Devourer, greedily waiting to judge a group of ancient Egyptians to see if their hearts weighed more than feathers.

Without knowing it, Mace clutched at his chest, as if protecting what it contained.

///// CHAPTER FOUR

Juan Pablo Garcia leaned against the alley wall of the corner market, one foot propped up against the red bricks, so that his knee stuck out into the dark alleyway. Beyond the edge of the shop, the alley opened up, and the road stretched off to the edge of the cliffs overlooking the Pacific Ocean near the bottom of South America.

The balmy sea breeze shifted, and Juan Pablo glanced left into the darkness beyond the last streetlamp, waiting for his mysterious challenger to arrive.

A couple dozen friends from school were milling about

in the shadows nearby. His uncle, the Punta Arenas Chief of Police, sat smoking a cigar in his parked cruiser with the engine off but the radio on, blocking cars from turning onto the alleyway. This late at night, there was no traffic to worry about. Most of Juan's fans were far away at the cliffside finish line, playing their music loud enough on their car stereos that Juan Pablo occasionally heard the wind carrying a distant tune. The rowdiest among them would be throwing empty glass bottles over the edge of the cliff to hear them smash against jagged rocks in the darkness and sea foam below.

His uncle's radio was broadcasting the live TURBO race happening in the Italian Alps. It was tomorrow morning in Italy. The announcer described a beautiful late-spring day there, as the course wove through green-carpeted valleys and the high, snow-capped peaks and alpine lakes.

The names Renegade and *Trailblazer* kept repeating on the radio. Apparently, the unstoppable wonder kid was crushing it again, coasting to another win with ten final reps to go. The hundred-lap race was entering its third hour. Katana was causing him constant headaches, but Mace Blazer kept making up time in the air and coming out ahead.

If Renegade won this race, it would mean an automatic berth in the Prix. He'd be the first 'naut to ever qualify so early in the season. He had already announced that if he won he'd take the next few races off, just to rest up.

Juan Pablo was fine with that.

He liked Renegade. He loved the idea that a kid was out there causing adults across the globe to foam at the mouth. Driving adults crazy by driving crazy. There was a poetry to it. But he was growing bored of Mace Blazer at the same time. The kid was dominating everything about the sport. It was impossible to turn around and not see or hear about him. And worse, Blazer seemed to know it. You could see it in his eyes. Juan Pablo wondered if all the fame and attention was truly deserved.

Katana should ditch her dicer, Juan thought. *She'd be creaming everyone if she didn't have to dork around on helicopter routes. Put Renegade in his place.*

A text came in from a pal waiting at the cliffs.

When are we starting?

He thumbed a response.

No idea. But I'm hungry. I want to get this over with.

Juan Pablo whistled to his cousin, the son of the police

chief, and beckoned him over. Juan Pablo liked to be alone before he raced, and folks knew not to bother him unless he needed something. At sixteen, Raul was a year older than Juan Pablo, but he knew the bellies of cars as well as any pro mechanic in the southern hemisphere and had been hunched over the open hood of Juan Pablo's ride, finely tuning engine components. Raul and Juan Pablo shared a brief buddy handshake. They spoke and texted in Spanish, though both of them knew English well enough to have used it. Mastery of English had come easily with a childhood following business-owning parents all around South America.

"How's she look?" Juan Pablo asked Raul.

"Perfect. She's ready to race."

They were referring to Juan Pablo's souped-up Mitsubishi Eclipse. She now had more than *three times* the horsepower of the factory model. Juan Pablo had never lost a race with her. Everyone in Punta Arenas—everyone south of the sixty-eighth parallel, for that matter—had heard tell of his talent behind the wheel, and of the dangerous new form of street racing he had mastered.

Juan Pablo's rise to stardom as the fastest kid in Tierra del Fuego had been well-timed, what with the Gauntlet Prix passing through town at the end of this year. People thought he should race TURBO, but he wasn't interested. He liked street racing. It was rougher and less predictable, without so many annoying rules. Still, that hadn't stopped him from winning some VIP passes off a rich kid in a street race. *Maybe I'll even meet Mace Blazer in the flesh,* Juan Pablo thought.

Pro TURBOnauts were trickling into town to do their research and get the lay of the land. Juan Pablo had snapped a selfie with none other than Akshara Brahma of *Untouchable* last month, and he had seen *Velocity Raptor*'s Malcolm Veloz from across the central park a few weeks before that. Movie star Thaddeus Hightower, who'd played a TURBOnaut in films, had even been here scoping out villas to rent and had personally asked Juan Pablo about the best places along the routes where audiences would be watching the Prix.

And there was tonight, of course. This street race was proof that his name and his reputation were getting out there.

"Impatient," scoffed Juan Pablo. "Tell me about it. Speaking of which, where's this guy at? We're all getting tired of waiting."

Raul shrugged unhelpfully. "Don't look at me!"

"He's your contact. You set this up."

"I don't know. This dude who knows another dude who knows another dude shows up at my door with a bag of cash and a piece of paper with a date and time on it. And your name. He said you'd get double the cash if you beat his guy. That's all there is to it. You know as much as I do."

"Well, the date and time was yesterday, 11:30 p.m. It's after midnight. How long are we supposed to stand around like a bunch of idiots?"

Raul shrugged. "Then you got a giant bag of cash for doing squat."

"Not true. I could be at home watching the TURBO race."

On the police cruiser radio, the announcer was getting excited. Katana had overtaken Renegade and looked to be in a position to hold on to the lead for now. Chief Garcia laughed from his seat in the shadows. "The finish is gonna be good," he yelled across the alley. "I got money on the lady. You better not have me out here for nothing!"

"Patience, Tío. They're coming," shouted Juan Pablo. But he wasn't so sure.

And then two pairs of headlights turned into view far down the main road. They approached slowly and stopped at the alleyway. Chief Garcia turned on his car and moved it off the street to let them pass. Only the first car pulled forward. It was nothing special, a beat-up Toyota with salt and rust damage. The windows were down, and Juan Pablo could only see one guy inside.

"That's him," Raul pointed out. "The contact who set this up."

The man drew even with Juan Pablo. He had a beard. His expression was guarded. "Are you going to do this?" he asked. No introductions. No small talk.

"I'm ready," Juan Pablo said. "Start line is right there. Have your guy pull even with my car. You going to stay here or skip ahead to the finish?"

"I'll be at the finish line. You win, you get another bag of money."

"Okay," Juan Pablo said. "You know my uncle, yeah?" He indicated the police chief with his chin.

"I know your uncle."

"No funny stuff, then, right? He'll be at the finish too. I win, you pay up."

The man nodded and started to drive away.

"Hey!" Juan Pablo called out. "Who am I racing?"

The man snorted and shrugged. "I dunno. Just following instructions, same as you." He drove away, disappearing in the dark in the direction of the distant cliffs and the finish line.

"Dude, what is going on?" Raul asked.

"This is weird," Juan Pablo agreed.

The other car began to pull forward. It came into the light of the streetlamp. Raul and the police chief whistled together. All the lingering friends gathered around.

Juan Pablo had never seen anything like it. Was it even a car? It was on wheels, but . . . It almost reminded him of a trimorpher, but TURBO racers were rarely this futuristic-looking. It was like a cross between the Batmobile and a mini SR-71 Blackbird. No roof or windshield, but a tear-shaped glass canopy. A hint of wings? Mostly tucked in but ready to spring forth with a simple command? Juan Pablo was imagining it. The contours were simply for curb appeal.

The vehicle rolled forward and halted level with the Eclipse on the start line.

Folks circled around it, murmuring. Chief Garcia extracted himself from his cruiser and came up beside the vehicle, crossing his arms and whistling again. Someone said, "Juanpa's toast!" and laughed. Everyone laughed, the police chief loudest of all.

"What's she got under the hood? Thousand horse-power?" someone quipped.

"That's for the space agency to know and for Juanito to find out," the chief said.

Everyone laughed harder. Juan Pablo's heart skipped a beat.

"All right, guys, back off. Give 'im some space." Juan Pablo shooed his friends away like they were annoying sea gulls and circled the car himself.

"Hey," he tried, waving toward the sleek, black glass. All the car's surfaces were glossy and smooth, reflecting the dull yellow light of the streetlamp in beautiful, shapely arcs. "What do you call this thing? What kind of engine does it have?"

No answer came from within.

Juan Pablo tried again. He walked up to the driver's side and tapped on the glass. He tried to peer into the interior, but the canopy was opaque. "Hey, we gonna shake hands before the start, or what?"

No response.

"Or what, I guess," said Raul.

"Whatever." Juan Pablo turned his back to the other

driver. "Let's get this over with." He circled around the front of his own car while his friends cheered.

"We can still catch the end of the TURBO race," the chief of police said, hustling back to his cruiser. "Take him down!" he encouraged his nephew. "But, Juanito—don't be stupid. I don't want to be calling my brother to tell him his son is fish food."

Juan Pablo's friends piled into their cars and peeled away, racing to take up spots at the finish. Raul jumped into the cruiser and disappeared into the dark with his dad.

Juan Pablo's heart was thumping as the dust settled around the starting line. He entered the Eclipse and slammed the door shut quickly, already going through his mental check-list. Seat belt. Headlights. Ignition. A couple revs of the engine to wake his baby up. She sounded smooth. Powerful. Hungry. Juan Pablo glanced over at the other vehicle, hoping to glimpse anything new. But the driver within gave him nothing.

"I'll just have to go fast," he said aloud. *But don't forget your stop mark*, he thought nervously. *You know your brake-point. You're going to have to really toe the dead zone with this guy, right up to the last fraction of a second.*

The other vehicle answered Juan Pablo's engine test with

the roar of its own pistons. He could feel its power penetrate into the Eclipse interior, right up through his rib cage. Juan Pablo let off his own pedal to hear the mystery vehicle. It had a clean growl, and he knew he was up against the steepest competition he'd ever faced. V-12 at least. It could easily have a 720-horsepower engine. And yet it idled like a happy kitten on a windowsill. That took some serious fine-tuning.

This road would be the great equalizer. Juan Pablo knew he wouldn't have a prayer against this modern predator on a stadium track. But the roads of Punta Arenas, one of the southernmost cities on Planet Earth, poised near the last habitable tip of a continent where the Atlantic Ocean and the Pacific Ocean meet, had decades-old roads abused by the harshest conditions. Horsepower was second to handling.

He turned the radio on. Usually during a race, he played "Eye of the Tiger" by Survivor. But the TURBO race in the Alps was still unfolding live, and Juan Pablo caught the excitement in the announcer's voice. With about a minute left in the race, Renegade had retaken the lead from Katana. A surprising late challenger, Italian Luca di Luca, was hot on their tails.

The speed and intensity of the broadcast was contagious.

Juan Pablo grew tightly wound in his seat, ready to spring from the line. The play-by-play on the race was better than any song. It felt like he was about to enter the TURBO match, go head-to-head with the wonder kid himself. He left the stereo on and let his blood course through his hot veins.

"THIS IS ANYBODY'S RACE, FOLKS, BUT BLAZER WANTS IT MORE. HE'S INCHING AHEAD ON THE INSIDE TRACK AND— OH WAIT! KATANA'S FOUND A BURST OF SPEED. WHERE WAS SHE KEEPING THAT? A LAST-DITCH ACE UP HER SLEEVE? IT MIGHT JUST BE ENOUGH!"

A traffic light, lying on its side up ahead in the street between the paths of the two race cars, activated to indicate that Raul and the others had reached the cliff. The traffic signal had been stolen from town ages ago, modified by Raul into a remote countdown device.

The light shone red then flashed yellow. Juan Pablo jammed the clutch down, let his other foot lightly off the brake, and gripped the stick shift.

Green.

Juan Pablo rocketed into gear and lurched powerfully off the start. The wheels gripped at crumbling pavement, spinning a rotation or two before catching. But this was normal;

Juan Pablo knew how to make it work. And he got the jump on the other racer! What a surprise! Half a second faster. An eternity for a race this short!

"AND KATANA'S RIGHT THERE. SHE'S BEEN RAVENOUS FOR AN OUTRIGHT WIN THIS YEAR, AND SHE LOOKS POISED TO FINALLY SEIZE A VICTORY. A LITTLE WOBBLE THERE, BUT SHE'S NOT LOSING GROUND. IT'S GOING TO BE A PHOTO FINISH."

Juan Pablo and his rival thundered away, escaping the reach of the last streetlight as they took to the open road leading to land's end. Beyond the headlights, Juan Pablo could see stars. A dim, waning moon illuminated the low clouds shrouding the tall, silhouetted mountains beyond the far shore of the ocean channel. The other vehicle was a constant, fixed image locked at his side. Everything else was a smear.

The other guy hit a pothole and swerved. *Maybe this dude's just another rich blowhard who thinks a fancy car is all it takes. . . .*

Mystery Man would find out soon enough that winning took more than brute horsepower. But Juan wasn't going to let off the pedal, not one bit.

The finish grew apparent in the distance, lit brightly by

all the headlights of the spectators' cars. Juan Pablo and the mystery driver were glued to each other. Juan Pablo had nothing left to give; he was at full speed. But he was feeling good. Even if he lost to this exciting new car, it would only be by fractions of a second. In the eyes of his fans, that would still win him praise.

"THEY'RE OVER THE LINE. IT'S A THREE-WAY PHOTO FINISH. FIRST, SECOND, AND THIRD, SEPARATED BY A RAZOR'S EDGE. *CATACOMB*'S LUCA DI LUCA WAS THERE AT THE HEAD OF THE PACK! IMAGINE IF HE SQUEAKED OUT A HOME-TURF WIN HERE, OUT OF NOWHERE? AGAINST THE HOTTEST 'NAUTS OF THE YEAR! WE'LL SEE. WE'RE STANDING BY."

A tumbleweed rolled onto the road. Juan Pablo's trained eye noticed the movement, and he dismissed the threat. Nothing would slow him now. Amazingly, though, the other vehicle faltered, slowing and veering to avoid the obstacle. Juan Pablo went right over the somersaulting weed, his eyes focused on the approaching finish. His challenger over-corrected, fishtailing and nearly careening off course. At such high speeds, the vehicle could flip!

Juan Pablo's eyes were everywhere at once. The finish: he had to brake the second he crossed it, but not an inch sooner. He kept glancing at the other vehicle, wondering if it was about to slam into the crowd. All his friends. His cousin. His uncle!

A stabilizing wing extended from the side of the car. Juan Pablo gasped. It *was* a morpher! He should've known and called the whole thing off! How could he beat a vehicle that wasn't afraid of the cliff? The race had been unfair from the get-go.

The Eclipse crossed the finish line. Juan couldn't tell who'd won. He slammed the brake pedal, yanked up on the emergency brake. The cliff was coming at him way too fast. His wheels skidded. His car spun, facing backward. Nothing he could do but sit it out. He slowed. Slowed some more. The other car had both wings out now. It could simply fly off once the ground dropped away. Not fair!

Finally, Juan Pablo came to a stop with a hard jolt. His rear left tire had crossed over the cliff's edge, and the bottom of the car ground him to a halt with only inches to spare. He'd never come so close to actually plummeting before!

The morpher clipped a parked car with its far wing. It whipped around, out of control, and sailed off the edge of the world.

"No!" Juan Pablo shouted.

He leaped from his vehicle to watch. He was just quick enough to catch a glimpse of the shadowy morpher tumbling. Tumbling. And then it struck the wave-wracked boulders at the base of the cliff and exploded.

Juan Pablo was thrown backward as the fire blast reached up to engulf him.

He lay flat on his back as the silence returned. Waves crashed far below against the rocks, indifferent to all that had just happened.

"MACE BLAZER!" the announcer suddenly shouted from the stereo in the teetering Eclipse. "HE'S DONE IT AGAIN. A WIN BY THE SMALLEST OF MARGINS! BUT IT'S A WIN. HALF-WAY THROUGH THE SEASON, AND HE'S ALREADY QUALIFIED FOR THE PRIX! CHILE AND ARGENTINA, TIME TO UNROLL YOUR WELCOME MATS FOR THIS YEAR'S FIRST CONFIRMED CONTENDER."

"You're okay!" Raul shouted.

"Doing better than that guy," Juan Pablo glanced toward the ocean. Across the channel were the tall, snowcapped mountains of Tierra del Fuego. A few hundred miles beyond that, the real end of the Earth: Antarctica.

Juan Pablo's friends helped him to his feet, and they watched the smoldering debris. There wasn't much to see from up here. It was dark far below, and the fire in the core of the craft, fed by ultra-performance rocket fuel, was doused by the high spray of angry waves. "Did he make it?" Juan Pablo asked. "Did you see him eject?"

Raul and the others shook their heads. "The canopy came off. But . . . we didn't see anyone escape. It happened so fast. It's so dark."

Chief Garcia ran up, huffing and holding his hat on as he fought the updraft flowing over the cliff. He leaned over the edge, wincing and shaking his head. Behind him was the quiet bearded man who had been the intermediary for the mystery driver. Pale-faced, he looked hesitant, confused and concerned.

"Let's get some men down there," the police chief commanded. "I have to call this in. But I wasn't here to start with, you all understand? And neither was Juan."

Heads nodded their agreement.

"Get that car on solid ground," added the chief, pointing at the Eclipse partially dangling over the edge.

Chief Garcia whipped around on the bearded man. "Who

was that guy?" he demanded. "We need to know who he was."

The man shook his head. "We never met in person. I know he wasn't local." He handed the bag of money over to the chief. "Sorry I can't help. But maybe this'll answer some of your questions. As evidence, I mean."

"Get out of my face!" The chief snatched up the bag and barked orders.

Everyone got to work. By the time backup police cruisers and the fire truck arrived, Juan Pablo was driving toward town along a quiet side road with Raul by his side. A bag of money rested in Raul's lap.

"Dad said this belongs to you," Raul explained.

"Toss it in the back. We'll need it for repairs." The Mitsubishi was handling sluggishly, limping along and pulling to the right. This matchup had bruised her badly.

"Did I win?" Juan Pablo asked now that things had slowed down.

"I think you did, Juanpa. I'm sure someone captured it on video. But all eyes were on that thing as it started morphing. I'll see if someone got a good angle on it."

"Don't," Juan Pablo waved him off. "I don't care. Just

glad I'm alive. That was crazy."

"Yeah. What *was* that?" Raul asked, trying to make sense of it all.

"We'll find out more when they recover the body, I'm sure," Juan Pablo said. "Your dad's good at his job when he wants to be."

But the next afternoon when Juan Pablo finally woke up and ventured into his apartment kitchen, his uncle was sitting at the table. There was a tremble in his hands as Juan Pablo asked him for an update. The chief shook his head, his eyes downcast. "No," he said. "Never found a trace of the driver. Jet fuel incinerated everything. I collected a sample to send to Santiago for DNA analysis, but it might've been charred floor matting, for all I know. By the time we got down there everything that wasn't metal was washed away. More like a meteorite impact site than a car crash."

"Nothing? Are you sure?" Juan Pablo pressed him.

The chief of police scratched his head. *"Nada."*

CHAPTER FIVE //////

Once again, it was race day.

Once again, the trimorphers were escorted by pit crews out to their starting positions—this time on the Rockingham Motor Speedway tarmac. The final countdown for the London 300 was on. The grandstands were filling up. Fans were milling about in parking lots, tailgating, or shopping for TURBO memorabilia in arena gift shops beneath the stands. The quiet before the roar seemed palpable as VIPs toured the pits and snapped close-up pictures of their favorite 'nauts. Seventy miles to the south, under scattered English clouds, fans throughout London were perched on folding chairs, from building tops to riverside boardwalks, growing noticeably more impatient, excited for the green flag to drop and for the race to zigzag along the River Thames, over the Tower Bridge, and throughout the city.

Once again, there was buzz about a mystery TURBOnaut entering the sport. Newbies almost always turned out to be duds, but exceptions—like Renegade and Katana last year—helped to fuel speculation.

And once again, Mace Blazer was giving his fans plenty to talk about.

But this time it was because *Trailblazer* was missing from today's lineup.

London would not be watching Mace defend his winning streak.

Instead, Renegade was sinking into a plush leather couch next to Dex and Melanie, in a side room of a downtown London Mazagatti dealership, waiting to film a car commercial. Mazagatti was an ultra-high-end luxury sports car company. With a base price of several hundred thousand dollars, their customized vehicles could sell for well over a million bucks each, depending on a client's upgrades.

The company wanted to use Renegade in an ad for their new Relativity EMC. And to lend an air of authenticity, and for marketing purposes, they wanted to film it live during an actual race.

While the film crew set up cameras and fussed over getting the lighting perfect, Mace took another sip of soda, watching the prerace unfold on TV. This was his first stint as a TURBO *spectator* in almost a year, and he hated feeling sidelined. But maybe Melanie was onto something by insisting he sit this one out. Everyone was discussing his absence— oddly making him feel all the more present.

His own smiling face was onscreen right now, accompanied by a list of racing stats. A reporter interviewed fans who shared their disappointment that Renegade was taking a breather.

"He's too busy going to museums with princesses and partying with his rich friends, I guess," one deflated kid lamented into the microphone.

That stung. Mace threw up his hands. "Ouch!"

"Don't worry about it," Melanie argued. "You're in the Prix. Only the best TURBOnauts have the luxury to pause on the road to the Glove. It adds to your legend."

"I'm not in this sport to market myself as some kind of legend. I'm in it because I love to win," Mace pushed back.

"Then what'd you hire a publicist for?" Melanie retorted.

Good question, Mace almost said.

"Hold on, TURBO maniacs," Jax Anders's voice blurted from the TV with growing excitement. "We're finally getting some details about the new contender in today's lineup. Hard to believe, but . . . yes, Hollywood A-lister *Thaddeus Hightower* is officially switching career tracks! The lead actor of numerous racing movies on the silver screen has formally announced he's going TURBO in real life. Not as a cryptic, but totally on the level."

"Whaaaat?" Mace said.

Dex frowned. "Rad Thad wants to be a real TURBOnaut? That's ridiculous."

"Does he have a new movie coming out?" Mace asked. "Sounds like a publicity stunt. Who's sponsoring him?"

Jax Anders kept talking, one hand to his ear as info was pumped into his headset. Various still shots and movie clips of Thaddeus Hightower flashed onscreen as Anders reported. "Rad Thad" was in his early thirties and had already starred in more than twenty blockbuster films. He'd stormed into

66

Hollywood after his early days of acting in sitcoms as a kid. He'd played a TURBOnaut in a series of movies about the sport a while back. Mace had always been first in line to buy tickets for those films. Cheesy and totally inaccurate, they nevertheless glorified the world of TURBO.

Hightower had been getting into trouble lately. His last few flicks had bombed, and he had recently been seen kissing a woman who wasn't his wife. A nasty divorce had followed.

"First we sanction a twelve-year-old boy to race in the pro league, fellow maniacs, and then this," Anders concluded. He paused for dramatic effect, tapping a pen ponderously on his glass tabletop. "The sport of TURBO is selling its soul."

"Wait a minute! Why are they bringing *me* into this?" complained Mace.

"Allowing a washed-up, hungover Hollywood darling to yank his flailing film career out of the gutter . . ." Jax Anders shook his head with dramatic flair. "This is going too far."

Anders straightened in his seat. "I'm being told we have exclusive footage of Hightower himself, reacting to his announcement. Let's listen in."

The host of the show was replaced with a full-screen image of the actor, close up, with a mic shoved in his face.

"Rad Thad" wore dark aviator sunglasses beneath a head of short, full-bodied black hair. He smiled smugly for the camera.

"We're really excited about this," Hightower explained, his voice practiced and as confident as any of the action heroes he'd portrayed. "This has been in the works for a while, and it just seemed like the right time to jump in the mix. I realize there are going to be haters out there. But I'm the real deal, and I look forward to proving myself."

"Do you think portraying TURBO legend Rex Danger on the big screen has helped prepare you for this new 'role'?" asked the off-camera reporter.

Hightower shrugged. "I dunno. It's probably more accurate to say I was drawn toward the role of Danger because of my love for TURBO. It's going to be really exciting to let the real TURBOnaut in me out for a spin here in London."

"Do you think you have a shot at placing this weekend?"

Mace threw a tortilla chip at the television. "Placing! He'll be lucky to finish at all. This isn't a movie."

Rad Thad gave the camera two thumbs-up. "I'm taking this seriously. Placing is the goal. We'll see. I'll tell you what, let's talk more after the race?" He gave the off-camera reporter a firm pat on the shoulder and left.

Mace's phone started ringing. He didn't recognize the number, so he let it go to voice mail. Then he got a second call, this one from Jax Anders's direct cell number.

"Don't answer that," Melanie instructed. Then her phone started ringing, too. "Don't worry!" she insisted to Mace. "It doesn't matter. Like you said: He'll be last and that'll be the end of it." The publicist answered her phone and walked out of the room, talking fast.

Dex laughed weakly. "Biggest movie star in the world. Thad Hightower thinks he's got a shot at placing."

The whole situation was genuinely laughable. But Mace wasn't amused. He knew how the TURBO media worked. This goofy publicity stunt would rule the rest of pregame coverage.

"I shouldn't have skipped this one," Mace grumbled. He asked Dex, "Is it too late for me to suit up? That guy needs that smug smile wiped off his face."

"Actually," Dex mused, "It's probably good you're not there. This is beneath you."

"Hmm," Mace said.

The Mazagatti commercial assistant entered the green-room. "Mr. Blazer, we're ready for you in makeup."

"Perfect timing," Mace said. He tossed the TV remote to Dex. "Anything to get my mind off this."

CHAPTER SIX //////

The London 300 was well underway. Trimorphers chased each other near enough to the Mazagatti dealership that Mace could hear and feel them rocketing overhead as the makeup crew finished fiddling with his face and hair. It was early enough that the pack hadn't yet separated into a long, trailing string. The swarm produced a deafening but infrequent interruption. Mace was feeling relaxed: with the race settling in, Rad Thad would be falling from last place to utterly left behind. His publicity stunt would quickly be forgotten.

"Done," the makeup lady declared, breathlessly impressed with herself as she gave Mace a last once-over. "I've done work for Mazagatti ads in the past, you know. They don't get to the top of the luxury car market without a keen eye toward every. Little. Detail."

The director's assistant ushered Mace out of the makeup room and down the hallway toward wardrobe. Dex intercepted Mace in the hall, letting out a deep, dramatic sigh. "Hightower's . . . not . . . sucking."

"What?"

"He's doing . . . good. I don't know what to say. We're a third of the way in and The Leading Man is holding steady around twentieth."

"Wait. Did you say Leading Man?"

"That's his registered race name. I'm not even going to tell you what he calls his trimorpher."

"What is it?"

"No. Really. I can't bring myself to say it."

"How's Aya doing?"

"She's in and out of first."

"Well, see? What's there to worry about?"

"He started dead last, Mace. He's . . . flawless. And he's getting faster."

"Whatever," Mace waved his crew chief off, battling a sudden wave of unexplainable anger. "Come on, Dex: it's a fluke. Anybody can catch an early break." The more he talked, the more he convinced himself of his logic. "These races are about stamina. He'll peter out before the end."

Dex wasn't convinced. "Maybe. But . . . so far this is different. Win or lose, they'll be talking about him."

Mace really didn't want to deal with this right now. "Bug me in an hour. Right now, I have a date with a tailored tuxedo."

He proceeded down the hall, where he was introduced to Germaine, the wardrobe guy. "Oh, your makeup is perfect! You look like a million dollars, kid!" Germaine exclaimed.

Mace wanted to scratch his head, but he knew it would cost him another hour of hairstyling. "They really captured my essence, didn't they?" he agreed.

The wardrobe guy came and went over the next half hour as he measured Mace and adjusted his tuxedo. He endlessly mixed and matched different bow ties, pocket squares, and cuff links.

"It must be hard for you to be here on a race day," Germaine told Mace while straightening his collar. "Especially with that actor doing so well. Here, try the blue pocket square with that."

Mace struggled to fold the kerchief into right angles. "How long ago did you check the standings?" he asked.

"Just now. Hightower's in *first*. Leading Man, indeed. You haven't heard?"

"Um," Mace said. He avoided the question, replying with his own. "Is Katana in second?"

"No idea. Too bad you're not there. Or maybe you dodged a bullet today." The guy gave Mace a stiff elbow nudge. "Head on out to the set. Ask for Dan Lorenzo. He's the director."

Mace's hand was unsteady, shaking, as he opened the door. He led himself onto the showroom floor, stewing over Germaine's comment: *"Maybe you dodged a bullet today. . . ."*

"Thad Hightower dodged a bullet today," he grumbled.

The showroom was spartan: nothing on the white, curvy walls save a giant, red Mazagatti logo, and very little furniture other than a few spread-apart waiting-room seats and slabs of polished concrete rising from the floor as tables. Three models of Mazagatti sports cars were proudly on display, each of them mouthwateringly gorgeous, sleek, alluring, and dazzling on their well-lit pedestals.

A red Spitfire i80 coupe, a black Phantom Illuminati 5, and a midnight-blue Relativity EMC.

Mace badly wanted to get behind the wheel of each of the three models, press the ignition, get that fix of power and custom engineering.

The people on set acknowledged Mace with nods and guarded smiles. They watched him watch the vehicles. Mace circled the nearest sports car: the coveted Relativity EMC. It was a fine specimen of muscle and pure sheen. The EMC's official slogan was projected onto the showroom floor from lighting focused up above: "Extravagance equals Merit times the speed of Confidence."

He reached out and put a hand on the hood, then felt along its contours. This was the real deal—no prop. Mace could feel its beating heart resting within. He could sense that it had never been driven before. Not one mote of dust wedged into the componentry. It felt tightly wound, but still Mace could sense the fine-tuning of the—

"Did we get that?" shouted the director, Dan Lorenzo, jarring Mace out of his trance. "No! Ah. We should have filmed *that*! That could have been the commercial! Did you see his *awe*? We should have captured his face."

Mace pulled his hand away and shared a look with everyone behind the line watching him. "I could do it again," he suggested.

"We can try again," the loud guy sitting in the director's seat finished, "but then you'll be *acting*. We should have snapped that first approach!"

"Mind if I slip inside?" Mace asked. "Maybe film me doing that?"

"Hey, Spielberg, let me do the directing," Lorenzo replied. "You'll get behind the wheel later. We don't want fingerprints everywhere."

Mace felt sudden disappointment. He really wanted to connect with the vehicle. He needed his fix.

"All right, Mace," Lorenzo instructed. "Here's your lines. Say them as you enter stage left, walk toward the camera, and open the door of the EMC. Action!"

Mace got right down to work.

"If you're like me, you have the confidence to seize what

you deserve. Remember: you've earned the Relativity EMC. Embrace that mathematical relationship . . . where extravagance is a function of what you're due."

Ten takes later, Lorenzo still wasn't satisfied. "Again!" he'd say. And Mace would try talking while walking toward the camera and opening the car door a different way each time. The sounds of the race came again and again, in waves now, as the morphers spaced out over London. Filming paused while the cameras softly rattled.

Melanie and Dex strode onto the set. Dex had his arms crossed. He looked dour. Melanie was shouting into her phone. Mace watched them between takes, growing nervous.

"All right, now you can slip inside," said Lorenzo. He reviewed the plan while using wild hand gestures. "We'll push the car forward while you're behind the wheel. You'll emerge outside. Camera pans up as the real morphers fly overhead. One continuous shot. We'll need every take we can get before the race is over."

Finally. Mace tuned the rest of the world out. Slowly, ceremonially, he opened the door of the Relativity EMC and eased himself inside.

The seat was low, and he took several seconds to calm his nerves while he adjusted it upward to its tallest, most upright setting. That was better. Now he could see the ground in front of the sports car's nose. He gripped his hands on the wheel at ten and two, and his mind whisked him away to a windy road along the English countryside where he imagined taking all the curves at a hundred miles an hour.

"Excellent!" crowed Lorenzo. Mace startled. He had forgotten he was being filmed. The director looked toward the back of the car. "Now roll him outside. Next wave of racers is approaching!"

Mace looked in his rearview. Two guys were crouching down, ready to push the Relativity from behind. "Wait," he asked, "you're going to push me? I can just pull forward." He hovered his hand over the ignition button, desperate to feel that singular thrill of its finely crafted engine coming to life.

The director shook his head. "No can do. Illegal. You don't have a driver's license."

"What?" Mace spat. "That's totally stupid."

"Rules are rules, kiddo. Don't look so hurt."

"Give me a break. I can drive anything. Anywhere."

"Sure, kid, but we don't want fumes accumulating indoors, anyway. Let's get started. We've only got time for a couple dozen live shots before the race finishes."

Mace sat in the car with the driver's window rolled down for what seemed like forever, being pushed back and forth in and out of the dealership. *This is humiliating,* he thought. Outside, trimorphers were constantly overhead, racing past as intermittent streaks, rocking the Relativity with their forceful wakes. Lorenzo was frustrated. No one had anticipated that the morphers would still be wet after rising out of the Thames a few blocks away. River water rained down on the car constantly. The poor crew scrambled to keep the exterior polished and dry.

Every couple of takes, Mace spotted a golden blur he'd never seen before. *That must be Hightower,* he reasoned. Though he hoped he was wrong. The gold morpher was clearly the leader. And each time it passed, the time it took for the next morpher to appear lengthened. The next racer wasn't Aya, because she was airborne elsewhere on a dicer route. He hoped she was staying ahead of Hightower once they met up on the other terrains.

Mace noticed Dex ducking in and out a few times over that next hour. Melanie never reappeared. Dex's mood seemed to evolve. At first he continued to look worried and maybe even miffed. But something like resignation—possibly even respect—began to appear in his eyes.

Mace wanted to tell him to stop coming around. The occasional unreadable glances weren't helping him focus.

The atmosphere over London grew quiet and still. A little at first, and then all at once. "That's a wrap!" Lorenzo bellowed. "Race is complete. I think we got enough takes to make something work."

Just then Dex came running out of the dealership and onto the exterior set. His eyes were wide as silver dollars. "Mace!" he called over. "You won't believe it."

His phone dinged. He stole a glance at the screen. A text from Melanie stared up at him. Mace saw the message as if it were flashing red, though that must have been his imagination.

I had to duck out. But call me as soon as you can. London has changed everything.

Mace slowly turned toward his crew chief. Dex's expression of utter disbelief was not a good sign.

I can't take this, he thought. He stayed in the Relativity as Dex came up beside him on the passenger side. "What is it? Spit it out. Did he win?"

"Mace," Dex leaned in through the passenger window. "It's not just that. I . . . can't explain. You have to see for your-self. Turn on your TV." He pointed at the EMC dash.

"This screen will play TV?" Mace asked.

"It's a Maz. Of course it will. Fire it up. Quick!"

Mace grinned. This was it: an excuse to feel the Relativity come to life. He reached over and pushed the ignition. The engine awoke with a sweetly delicious thrum. The sound it made was deceptively quiet and patient, for all the power Mace could feel churning beneath the hood. He started to feel calmer. This was all he needed—just a taste of fine engineering—to remind him of his center.

"That feels really nice," he noted.

"Pay attention," urged Dex. "Turn on your display. Go to *TURBOWORLD.*"

Mace navigated the display. In a daze, he sank into his seat, reading the all-caps chyron scrolling along the bottom of the *TURBOWORLD* broadcast.

RAD THAD WOWS! THE LEADING MAN SASHAYS TO DEBUT WIN!

"Sashays to a win?" *Impossible.* He leaned forward, focused his eyes on the footage, and his heart rate doubled—tripled. The Leading Man's trimorpher was painted all gold. He heard the broadcaster use the vehicle's name for the first time.

"*I'd Like to Thank the Academy*?" Mace parroted, barking to Dex.

Dex was still leaning in through the passenger window. "I know. It's all insane."

The name of the trimorpher was obnoxious, but that wasn't the problem.

The problem was how the vehicle handled.

Mace felt the blood leaving his face as he examined the clips. *I'd Like to Thank the Academy* was an unshakable missile on all three terrains. It cut a line through the crowd of other trimorphers, weaving and swaying up through the ranks with near-perfect anticipation. It edged in on other drivers with breathtaking precision. Thaddeus rarely slowed. He never wobbled. Right from the gate, he made the other racers at the back of the pack look like they were engaged in a downhill derby with box cars. There was just no denying the simple genius behind the handling.

The finish was far from a blow-out. Katana took a respectable second, considering. She'd followed The Leading Man across the checkered line a little less than a second later. And other highly ranked TURBOnauts were close behind. *Untouchable* and *Velocity Raptor. Vertigo, Tsunami, Prometheus*, England's own *Cauldron*.

There was only so much one could physically do to blow past a veteran 'naut. But Hightower had done it.

Mace was witnessing near perfection. He wanted to hate what he was watching. He should at least feel jealous. But his overwhelming reaction to what he was seeing was frankly . . . admiration.

Melanie's right: this changes everything.

The admiration vanished, replaced with churning despair. A terrifying thought pierced his mind: *I don't know if I would've beaten this guy. Maybe I did dodge a bullet today.*

Shaken, Mace squeezed at his temples. *Don't think that. Of course you can beat him. Everyone in that race was shell-shocked. It threw them off their game. We'll all be ready for it next time.*

"Hey, Mace!" Lorenzo stormed forward toward him.

"Turn that off! You're not supposed have it on."

Mace rolled his eyes. "I haven't gone anywhere. Just watching the news. Give me a minute?"

Lorenzo stopped. He frowned but backed away. "Whatever. I'm not your dad. It's the dealer who'll have your head."

Thaddeus Hightower himself appeared onscreen. Mace forgot the director and turned up the volume in the car.

Hightower wore large aviator sunglasses, mirror-plated in gold, and an enormous grin that bared his blindingly white teeth. His short black bangs dripped with sparkling wine that had been shaken and sprayed on him by his pit crew. "Here we are!" he beamed, speaking into a hoard of mics, looking from one unseen camera to the next. "I like to go big—what can I say? There were a lot of good racers out there today. A lot of 'nauts with tremendous heart. I think, really, people weren't expecting much out of me. But that's what I enjoy doing: I love rocketing past people's expectations."

All around him, amid a new spray of erupting sparkling wine, a gaggle of scantily clad girls swooned as they crowded in, their arms outstretched, trying to reach close enough to touch him while big dudes in dark sunglasses kept them at bay with sternly crossed arms. *Thaddeus! You're the raddiest!"* they hollered in unison.

"No way," Mace said, his fists tightening around the steering wheel.

"Was this a fluke, Thad?" someone asked. "Can you do it again?"

"I told you we'd make a splash today." He nodded. "Everyone thought this was a huge joke, but I came out here and did what I knew I could do. I'm looking forward to repeat performances. It feels good to win."

"What about Renegade?"

"Who?" Hightower laughed his trademark laugh, but Mace could detect an underlying impatience on his features. "What about him? Too bad he bailed today. Makes you wonder what he was afraid of."

Mace punched off the display. He squeezed the steering wheel and growled at Dex. "The reporters are going to have a field day with this, all the way until the next race, over and over again: 'Can you knock The Leading Man off his game, Renegade?' *He's* the one who needs to prove himself. Not me."

Lorenzo reasserted himself into Mace's line of sight. "All right, Blazer. You want to drive that thing? Why don't you pull it around and park it back inside before the execs hud-dled over there wise up?"

"Right on," Mace said. "You got it." He pressed the brake with one foot and pushed down the clutch with the other. He shifted into first and started crawling forward.

Mace's heart skipped. He felt a flash of heat rise up his back. When he let off the brake, the horsepower beneath his feet stretched awake. He felt the EMC's sixteen-cylinder, four-turbo-charger purr coursing through his legs and up through the cooled-leather seat to massage his back and shoulders. The impulse to feel how it handled was irre-sistible. And why not? He'd missed the thrill today of sudden acceleration, sharp turns, tight passages, and near misses. He craved a quick sprint. And right now, he was being afforded the chance to get one.

Pull it around and park it back inside, Lorenzo had said.

But he hadn't specified how large a loop to make. He glanced at the herd of people in shiny ties off to the side. They weren't paying attention to their precious EMC at all.

"What about Renegade?"

"Who?"

"I need to clear my head," Mace told himself. *Just one*

city block. They'll forgive me. He began to roll forward, slowly at first, and then faster.

"Mace," Dex warned.

"Shh. I'll be fine. Just one block." He winked at Dex, and then rolled off the lot, leaving his wingman behind.

////// CHAPTER SEVEN

He pulled forward along the dealership asphalt and immediately felt the Relativity EMC's kick. This thing was spring-loaded, ready to launch.

Bystanders started pooling up on either side of the darkly tinted vehicle. They pointed, murmuring excitedly to one another. Phones came out and their cameras were directed at the EMC.

See? Back in the spotlight, Mace thought with a certain glimmer of satisfaction. The crowd couldn't tell who he was;

they were looking at the car. But still . . . he was giving them something to talk about.

"Extravagance equals merit times the speed of confidence," he told himself in a low whisper, imagining Melanie's approving nod. "I've earned this."

The Relativity had six speeds, could go from zero to sixty in 2.1 seconds, and could brake on a dime. If it handled anything like *Trailblazer* in roadster form, he'd have no problem piloting it.

Dan Lorenzo was shouting, his voice muted through the nearly airtight cabin. "Mace! Come back here!" He glanced in the rearview and spied the director trotting toward him.

"You going to do this?" he asked his reflection.

He answered his own question with a tap on the gas pedal. "Remember," he told himself. "They drive on the left here."

The EMC entered traffic with a jolt. A car came out of nowhere, screeching to a halt and causing Mace to brake. He let out a nervous laugh. "Cross traffic. That's a thing." He gave the hot rod some gas, almost rear-ended a black taxicab. He remembered his seat belt and frantically reached for it and fastened it. The click came just as traffic lurched forward.

He was off, gunning down the avenue past two black taxicabs and a Mercedes. The road ahead was empty, and he pushed forward, craving acceleration. He braked sharply, stopping with traffic at a light midway down the city block. As expensive a car as this was, the EMC *did not* handle quite as sharply as *Trailblazer*. He idled at the red light and caught his breath, absorbing just how different city driving was.

"Remember to give yourself a little extra wiggle room," he cautioned.

When the green light came, Mace punched the gas—and nearly rammed into the back of a Volvo. He slammed the brakes hard, jerking painfully against his taut chest restraint. He checked his side mirrors, preparing to dart into another lane, but a line of red double-decker buses and black cabs to either side was bumper-to-bumper, moving forward at a snail's pace.

"Stay in your lane," he jokingly scolded himself.

The Volvo inched forward. Mace followed, revving the engine. Heads turned. Comfortably hidden behind dark glass, he relished the secret attention.

The display screen on the dash flickered alive. Dex's frowning face appeared front and center. Dan Lorenzo glowered at him from over his shoulder. "Come on, Mace. You've had your fun. Knock it off and bring it back."

"Wow," Mace exclaimed, smiling. "Live video feed? I feel like James Bond."

"One scratch!" Lorenzo threatened, looming nearer, "and we're all in deep trouble. Turn it around before the dealer realizes you're AWOL. I'm not kidding. He'll have your head—and mine."

"I'm just going to Trafalgar," Mace promised. "I'll slingshot through the roundabout and zoom right home."

"Make it snappy," Lorenzo growled. "I can't protect you if they find out about this."

Traffic slowed suddenly again. Mace's stomach climbed into his throat. He veered into the emptier lane just in time and whipped past another black cab. *God, why are these streets so narrow and crowded? If only this were Colorado!*

A busy intersection was coming up. Mace saw an opening just wide enough to punch through and seized the moment.

A double-decker going full speed through its green light missed sideswiping him by inches.

Lorenzo popped back onto his screen. "Mace. They know. The owner says if you're not back here in ninety seconds they're tearing up our contracts. You've got me on the hook, here, too, damn it."

"A minute and a half?" exclaimed Mace, downshifting. "That's a lifetime."

"You know what?" the director said to someone out of view. "Set up the camera, snap him coming back. If I'm gonna hang for this, we're gonna get the footage, at least."

Mace grinned. "Good idea. I'll give you a shot to remember." He dodged slower traffic constantly, making a million adjustments. Rivals on the track were always going the same speed as he was—okay, a little slower. But dodging congested, crawling clunkers was an entirely new challenge. "No one out here realizes they're part of my race." He laughed.

"Dude, I don't like this," said Dex. "I think you should lay off, man. Your luck's going to run out."

The EMC picked up more speed. "Easy for you to say. D'you know how much that contract is worth?"

"No. But I bet it's less than a totaled Mazagatti."

"I know what I'm doing, Dex." *Merit times the speed of*

confidence. "Luck doesn't enter the equation. Let me concentrate."

The downtown London boulevard, lined on either side by tall stone buildings that formed canyon walls, became a familiar abstraction, reminding Mace of the streak of stadium seating on a closed-course speedway. *Now* he was getting his fix.

He moved to the center of the three lanes, just in case some unsuspecting pedestrian decided to jaywalk.

Mace was aware: *You could kill someone.* His eyes were sharp and focused, though. No obstacles were present—even the margins were clear. He had to make up time, and this was the time to do it. He didn't slow.

Left turn coming up. Mace waited as long as he could before decelerating, then drifted onto the new street and found himself snagged in another morass of cars. He started nudging ahead using the gap between lanes as if he were a motorcyclist. The black cabs didn't budge, but the normal cars gave way, providing him space to maneuver. Mace wasn't sure why, but he pressed his advantage and overtook the cabbies on the inside lane.

Melanie Vanderhoof's voice echoed: *People will give you the respect you demand.* "Ain't that somethin'?" he marveled.

"Sixty seconds," Lorenzo warned.

Mace was forced to veer right and conform to a logjam of bus traffic. Then he cut sharply in front of a driver to win over the inside lane and made a hard left turn onto the Trafalgar roundabout.

He accelerated, weaving effortlessly forward through cars that were obeying the speed limit around the circle. He swirled with merging traffic several lanes thick. Double-deckers swarmed. Mace glimpsed his own face on a London 300 bus advertisement. He wove through the metal maelstrom and kicked back out on the correct off-shoot lane with extra velocity, like a rocket ship whipping into deep space after making a moon pass.

The path opened up ahead, and he took full advantage, accelerating rapidly. When it was time to make the sharp turn onto the final straightaway, Mace glanced in his rearview. Traffic was thicker behind than it was ahead. The coast was clear, and he took a confident turn.

He found it easy to identify the fastest lane and to switch lanes when it was clear a slowdown was imminent. *Why am I so good at this?* he wondered.

The Mazagatti dealership was just around the next bend. Mace ground to a crawl behind a produce truck that was moving forward but in no hurry whatsoever. He agonized over whether or not he should quickly jog into the right lane and overtake the truck, but he decided to stay where he was. The other lanes were slow, too, and Mace didn't want to be stuck, unable to merge back to the left with the turn coming up. He waited it out. The tall truck continued straight at the intersection.

"Twenty seconds," Lorenzo growled. "They're not joking around."

Cameras are rolling. Finish strong. Mace floored it. He shifted, gave the EMC more juice—

His chest exploded with a pulse-pounding stab of horror.

Directly ahead, Mace glimpsed a woman pushing something in the middle of the street.

Watch out!

He swerved, flying up on the sidewalk. He missed killing

the woman by inches. But ahead, with its hazard lights flashing, was a parked white delivery van, its nose directly facing him.

"No, no, no!"

The white hood of the van filled his windshield. Mace jackhammered the brake and swerved, but it was no use.

Take it back! Take it all back!

And then Mace Blazer went from sixty to zero in no time flat.

The airbag opened—Mace watched it balloon outward and fill his vision—and he remembered nothing else.

CHAPTER EIGHT //////

WATCH OUT!

Mace swam awake, and for the first time in—*How many days has it been?*—he left his eyes open.

White foam ceiling tiles and star-shaped sprinkler heads greeted his vision. An IV stand with a half-full bag of clear fluid loomed over him. The room was quiet, but muffled sounds near the closed door hinted at a busy, crowded hallway beyond.

He'd been aware that he was in a hospital room. He had

memories of getting here. Snapshots. Glimpses from the past several days. Plane rides. Parents, pale faces tear-streaked. Dex. Aya. Nurses and doctors towering over him. Echoes of dull discomfort. More flights. Outbreaks of searing pain. But nothing was connected.

What happened? I don't remember!

There was a woman. Pushing . . . a cart?

White van.

He didn't want to know the whole story. His mind had preferred to escape into darkness, where there was no pain, no nightmares—

"Dude, I don't like this."

"I know what I'm doing, Dex."

—and no responsibility.

But it was time to wake up and face reality.

I'm alive. I didn't die. That, at least, was good. *But WHAT happened?*

He felt as stiff as a four thousand-year-old mummy and he had a sideache to end all sideaches. His nose itched, but it was no mystery why: white bandaging covered the front of his face.

He stirred to improve his view, testing his stiff joints. His left hand wouldn't budge at all, and the effort to raise his right arm sent white-hot pain along his side and chest. He barked in sudden agony, which made him cough, and the pain flared.

"Mace, are you awake?" he heard his mom say. She rose into view beside the bed.

"Mom," he attempted to sign. But the effort of trying to lift his thumb to his chin awarded him a new round of pain.

I can't talk to her! he thought with a twinge of dread. *What have I done?*

"I'm sorry, Mom." His voice was gruff and parched. His vision filled with tears.

"Don't worry, Mace," she signed. "You'll pull through. You're going to be okay. Do you know where you are?"

He shook his head.

"You're in Denver. What's the last thing you remember?"

Mace strained his thoughts until he found an answer. He had to spell it out with his right hand. "The commercial. London."

But there was more: *A woman in the street?*

Mom wiped away tears. "It's okay that you don't remember. You got a concussion. The doctor says it's normal for people to lose memories from before a crash."

Now she wiped tears away from *his* eyes. She leaned in close and embraced him as tightly as she dared. "My angel. I'm so happy to have you back."

"What happened, Mom?" he asked.

Dad entered the hospital room, overjoyed to find Mace awake. Dad wasn't good at lip reading, since he had been deaf since birth, and Mace was finding it difficult to communicate to him without reverting to finger spelling. Mom had to translate for Mace. This would have seemed amusing in other circumstances.

"I was in an accident," Mace guessed.

His parents nodded.

"The race car you were in," explained Mom. "You took it out on the streets."

Mace remembered: *Just one city block.*

"A minute and a half? That's a lifetime."

White van.

But everything else was a blank.

Dad signed to him. "The airbag saved your life, but it caused the injuries. Your left arm and your wrist are smashed, and you broke four ribs. Your nose was broken. They had to sew up your spleen. They put metal screws in your arm. You almost died, Mace."

"I'm sorry," Mace said, realizing just how close he had come to not being here anymore. He had no memories of an accident. Except for . . . a woman and a cart. And a van. But he remembered wanting to take the EMC out, knowing he wasn't supposed to. He understood that this situation was his own fault. He repeated it: "I'm so sorry."

"It'll be okay," Dad answered. "You'll be okay."

The woman in the road . . . "Did anyone else get hurt?" Mace asked, a sudden panic enveloping his thoughts.

"No," Dad reassured him. "Your driving actually saved lives. That's what they're saying."

Mace searched his mind.

Mace swerved, flying up on the sidewalk. He missed the woman and . . . and whatever it was she had been pushing.

The memory . . . more details threatened to unleash on him. He shoved it all away.

"How much trouble am I in?" Mace was fairly certain the answer was, "A ton." Just thinking about it brought new tears of regret and shame to his eyes.

"Hard to say," Mom said, brushing his cheeks again. "The van was parked illegally. The mother was jaywalking. Dex recorded all the conversations on his phone. It's obvious the business owners were threatening you—which means they pressured you to go fast. And the director actually set up cameras to benefit from the 'stunt work' he directed you to do. It's all being settled. Don't worry."

Settled? Mace thought. Relief washed over him. But . . . *mother jaywalking?*

"You're being cited with driving without a license," Dad signed. "Everything else is under seal."

"It's going to be okay, Mace," reassured Mom.

He took a deep breath, held it, accepting the pain in his ribs . . . and then let it out. The truth was: there was no one else to hold accountable. The decision to take the EMC onto the streets belonged to Mace alone.

"I know what I'm doing, Dex." Merit times the speed of confidence. "Luck doesn't enter the equation. Let me concentrate."

"No." He pushed the rest away and buried it deep.

//////////////////////////

102

The next morning, his meds were adjusted. He managed to stay awake all afternoon. Word came down that he could be discharged in a couple days.

"You're doing well," the doctor told him. "You have an athlete's body, Mace. No doubt about it. Go get comfortable in your home. Keep mending at this rate, and you'll be cleared for competition in time for the Great Lakes."

The Great Lakes All-Star Charity Run. Mace leaned back and let loose a deep sigh. It was the perfect race to have on the docket following an injury: a Prix qualifier, but an easy course, with straightforward terrains—and only two hundred laps. He could do it wearing a sling. He could do it blindfolded, really. By the time his body got tired and achy, it'd be over! He could make it work, but . . .

. . . *blinking hazard lights.*

White van.

I'm going to die.

Mace was suddenly drowning in the terror of it. It felt like falling off a cliff in a dream . . . but never waking up before the ground came.

He closed his eyes, holding further memories back. The dread passed, but . . .

He felt nauseated. "I need a bucket," he told the doctor.

The doctor produced a red biohazard bag, and Mace used it.

Over the years, many 'nauts have ended their careers after crashes. Mace had always wondered why they'd throw everything away like that, but now he thought he could sympathize.

How can I go back to that life? he thought.

"Because it's what you love," he said out loud when he was alone.

He nodded to himself. *Yeah.* Broken bones? Punctured organs? Who cares? He had lived. And he would get better. Risk was part of the sport, and he'd never wavered, never worried before.

He had nothing to fear. He was a pro.

Mace kept telling himself that. Over and over, until it stuck, like a gas pedal glued to the floor.

//////////////////////////

Melanie visited. "Glad to see you recovering so quickly," she told him, standing beside his bed with her arms cradling a leather portfolio. She pushed up her glasses with her free hand and then adjusted her earpiece. "Doctor says you'll be cleared for the charity run?"

"I don't know, Melanie, I'm not sure I'm ready—"

"I've got a strategy brief laid out for you." She reached into her binder and removed a white paper. "I've been around a lot of 'nauts over the years, and I get it: coming back from an accident can be no easy feat. But we'll get you back at the top by returning with a splash. Go big. Go strong. Take back the narrative. No remorse. No regrets. Ignore London."

"A splash?"

Melanie ignored him. "I think you should come out with a bold prediction next week: You're going to win the Great Lakes. With your arm still in a cast! Doesn't matter if you do or not. It'll get folks talking. Then—"

"Is Hightower registered for it?"

Melanie drew in a deep breath. "Yes, he is."

"Then it *does* matter if I win or not. I can't have him crush me in our first matchup."

"Mace. The stakes are low. No one will fault you if you're not 100 percent. You have the perfect opportunity to get a feel for him, actually. You have nothing to lose."

Just my life, he thought.

"But if you perform well . . ." Melanie trailed off.

"I'll think about it," he told her. His breathing picked up. "I need to rest."

She pursed her lips, studying him. "Okay," she said. "But I'll make sure everything's in order for the charity run. I believe in you, Mace! Oh, before I go, I have Princess Vasko on hold. She wanted to offer you support."

"Olesya?" Mace asked. He tenderly sat up straight.

Melanie tapped her headset off and passed over her phone.

Mace put it to his ear. "Hello?"

"Mace? Hi. You gave me quite a scare! I'm beyond relieved to hear you'll fully recover."

"Um. Yeah. Thank you."

"That was a nice EMC you were driving. I hope you got to keep it, at least. Break it, you buy it, as they say."

"Well, I haven't seen it, or any of the videos going around. But I'm guessing it wouldn't look so pretty in my garage."

The princess laughed. Her voice was so peppy and enthusiastic. It made Mace smile. "I expect to see you back racing this season. I simply must watch you and Thad Hightower compete. You'll do that for me? There's a ton riding on it."

"I think so," Mace ventured. "I'll try."

"You better. I need you to. And, oh, I'll be making a donation to the school your parents are starting during the charity run."

"Oh, thank you." Mace thought of something. His eyes lit up. "Can you do me a favor? Talk to my crew chief, Dex. Melanie can put you in touch. He has some questions for you."

"Sure. Anything. Just get back in there, Renegade! 'Kay?"

"Yeah. I'm gonna do my best."

"Do better than that. My dad's coming. Better go! *X*'s and *o*'s," she said, and disconnected.

Dex showed up later that afternoon. He placed his cowboy hat on the tray table teeming with flower bouquets. Mace managed to sit up enough to give his crew chief a fist bump.

"Nice look you're sporting." Dex used a spread hand to indicate the bandaging covering Mace's nose.

"I may have to go back to living behind the visor," said Mace.

"Naw. You'll heal up pretty." Dex sighed. The short silence was awkward. "You figured out how to grab the attention back from Hightower; I'll give you that."

"Well, Dex," Mace said, "I'm sorry I put you through it."

"I know." Dex took a deep breath. "It was pretty terrifying."

"I'm sorry," Mace repeated.

"Aya says hi, by the way. She's back in Japan. But she wanted to make sure you knew she was by your side in England, before they transported you home."

"I think I remember that. Barely. Tell her thanks if you get a chance."

"I will. Hey, so, I'm just going to say this. My talk with Olesya went really well. Thanks for finally connecting us. With her help, I think I'm going to be able to get out there with my own team soon, vie for the Glove myself."

"Dude"—Mace leaned back into the bed—"I'm really happy for you."

"I've got a trimorpher in production. She'll be a close cousin of *Trailblazer*, full disclosure." He shrugged shyly. "Gotta build what I know, right? I'm gonna start right away, at the Great Lakes."

"Seriously?" The true weight of Dex's announcement begin to press down on him. "Who's going to be my crew chief?" he asked the air.

"I wasn't going to leave you high and dry," Dex answered.

"I've already talked to Carson and his dad. They can take over for me if that's cool."

"Yeah, sure. I get it." Mace sighed.

"I hope you're not mad. Maybe I can put Hightower in his place. Even if I come up short—it's my opportunity to create some buzz. Are you . . . bouncing back for the Great Lakes?"

Mace's gut twisted, but he nodded. "I guess so. Doesn't really feel like I have a say in the matter."

"Well, good luck, man. I better get going. I've gotta lot to figure out before the run." They shared a final, gentle fist bump. "Get well soon, huh? But not so well that you make a fool out of me on Lake Erie."

"You'll do fine, Dex. You're a pro."

Dex put on his cowboy hat, gave his friend a gentlemanly nod.

Mace waited until he was gone to blink away the irritation that had been pooling up in his eyes.

///// CHAPTER NINE

Two weeks later, Renegade stood beside *Trailblazer*, his hand to his heart for the American national anthem—which was more awkward than usual since his left arm was in a sling—looking out at the expanse of Lake Erie from the shore of downtown Buffalo, New York. As the words of the anthem played over the loudspeakers, snippets of a nightmare looped in Mace's mind.

"... by the dawn's early light ..."

"No, no, no!"

The white hood of the van filled his windshield. Mace

jackhammered the brake and swerved right, but it was no use.

Take it back! Take it all back!

Mace scolded himself. "Knock it off, man."

The anthem finished, and cheers rose from the crowds. Mace leaned back against his roadster and squeezed his eyes shut for a moment. The typical noises marking the start of a race blended away. London kept edging into his mind, and he'd push it all away. He'd succeeded in not remembering the crash. It was important those memories stayed gone. "I need a distraction," he pleaded, glancing around as if one might appear.

One did.

A small mob approached. At the center of it: the utterly recognizable figure of Thaddeus Hightower, decked out in a golden flight suit and his trademark aviator sunglasses, gold-plated, shaking hands and grinning brightly. He was remarkably short in real life, Mace noted. But Hightower didn't seem to care. Mace wondered: had the guy changed his name to come across as taller?

He's a big deal, the voice of Melanie instructed him inside his head. *He knows it. That's how stars are supposed to act.*

I can't do it, Mace recognized. *I can't act that way. Even if I could a couple weeks ago, I can't now.*

Thad spent a minute with some lingering VIP guests and then noticed Mace propped against *Trailblazer*. He brushed away the huddle of fans and strode over to Mace.

"Hello there, Evel Knieval," Hightower said. "Look at you, all bandaged up, avoiding the media. Nice play."

Mace stood tall. He found himself at a loss for words.

"You up for this, Blazer?"

White van.

"Hey, man. Seriously. You okay? You look scared. Just being honest."

Mace finally found his voice. "Thad, don't you have a final inspection to oversee?"

The actor grinned broadly. "Listen, I'm glad you're okay. I'm glad you're back. I gotta give credit where it's due. You inspired me to come forward. I'll never forget the day in Cuba when you took your helmet off and revealed your true self. 'If he can do that, then so can I!' I said. And here we are!"

"That's great," Mace said, forcing up a smile.

You look scared. You inspired me . . . The guy had already gotten into Mace's head. He was like a burr clumped up in sheep's wool.

"Well, don't go soft on me. You've got a lot to prove today."

"Me? I don't have to prove anything," Mace told him. "I already know what's what. You're the one with something to prove."

"Whatever. Yawn. Say hi to Melanie for me, will ya?" Thad grinned.

"Gross. Leave her alone."

"Oh, no. I'm not . . . You do know that she was my publicist during the Rex Danger trilogy, right? That's how she broke into the TURBO industry. She never told you that?"

No. Melanie hadn't ever mentioned that. Mace stewed, balling his fist against his injured arm until it hurt.

"She's a brilliant strategist," Hightower admitted. "She made me who I am."

Of course, Mace thought. Look at him: a pompous, inconsiderate jerk. Totally full of himself. Melanie had been grooming Mace to be just like that. He'd never realized it before, but now it was clear.

And now another burr had nestled into his wool: *She made me who I am.*

A horn blared. The five-minute countdown had started.

Hightower hurried off, and Mace slipped into his cockpit. The Gerber son-and-father duo rushed beside him, going over the final checklist at a breakneck but practiced pace. Mace was fuming. But he was grateful. Hightower's bravado, and his revelation about Melanie, were exactly the sort of motivation he needed right now.

Put him in his place. Show him what's what.

The pit crew pushed the roadster up to Renegade's starting position on the track. Mace noted Dex right behind him. Parked in a silver-and-black *Trailblazer* look-alike named *Silverado*. He was clad all in black, a cryptic hiding his age just like Katana. "Good luck, Caballero," Mace muttered from behind his own visor. "You're going to need it."

"Racers, start your engines!"

Mace closed his eyes. His finger found the ignition automatically. *Trailblazer* roared to life. Mace felt a matching churning in his stomach. It wasn't nerves, though. It was terror. He suddenly felt sick. "Come on, Mace. Push through it."

He opened his eyes. He thought he was ready.

One of the three spectator megascreens within his field of view displayed his own image, larger than life, for the world to see. A ton of stats orbited his photo. He was back in the thick of it! His fans were counting on him! He wouldn't let them down.

And then the megascreen flashed, his picture replaced with a grainy, handheld phone's-eye-view of the London incident. The Mazagatti whipped through the busy streets, dodging cars. The shot was replaced by one from above, a news helicopter angle showing the blue EMC drifting sharply, at high speed, around the Trafalgar Square roundabout.

A chyron scrolled at the bottom of the footage: *BLAZER ESCAPES HIGH VELOCITY DEATH. AVOIDS INJURING OTHERS.*

He'd never seen playback from that day. The snippets up on the screen . . . they jogged everything lose, all at once.

Everything.

///////////////////////

"Twenty seconds," Lorenzo growled. "They're not joking around."

Cameras are rolling. Finish strong. *Mace floored it. He shifted, gave the EMC more juice—*

His chest exploded with a pulse-pounding stab of horror.

Directly ahead, in the middle of the street . . . was a woman pushing a baby stroller.

It was a blue jogging stroller, the kind with three big

wheels that you could shove while exercising. A tall coffee rested in the cup holder along the push bar. A small hand clutching a stuffed animal jutted out into Mace's line of sight. The animal was a polar bear. It danced in the toddler's out-stretched hand. . . .

Mace swerved. He missed the mother and child! But he flew up on the sidewalk . . . barreling toward a parked delivery van. . . .

"No, no, no!"

The white hood filled his windshield.

The airbag opened—

I'm dead. *The certainty was absolute.* And for what?

/////////////////////////

Mace lifted his visor and vomited all over the dash.

"Mace! Mace?" Carson Gerber's voice was frantic. "Do you copy? What's wrong?"

I almost killed a mother and HER BABY.

Mace looked up. He glanced around, baffled. He was alone on the tarmac.

The race had started. All of the other 'nauts were long gone. The crowd was silent. Mace knew that silence. It was called the end of the line. And it filled him with utter terror.

"Mace?"

He cleared his throat. "Ah. Just a sec."

"What's wrong?"

Mace took off his helmet. Vomit dripped from the chin guard. He wiped at his mouth with a sleeve. "I'm done. I'm coming in. I can't. I can't do this."

He was met with radio silence.

Mace guided *Trailblazer* back into the pit.

He exited the craft without looking at anyone. He bolted for the locker room on shaky legs.

In the corridor, someone stepped in his way. It was Melanie.

"It's okay, Mace. It's okay. We can still play this for sympathy. Your fans will—"

"Melanie," Mace stated, leaning against the wall with his head down, "I'm not playing this for anything. I almost murdered a baby!"

"Yeah, but you didn't—"

"Stop." He was feeling dizzy, but also embarrassed for her to see the mess on his flight suit.

"Are you repping Hightower at the same time as me?"

She stiffened. "That idiot. Did he say something to you?"

"Did you talk me out of racing the London 300 to make sure he could enter with a splash?"

"That's ridiculous. I'm not even going to dignify that with—"

"I'm finished with you."

"What?" she snapped.

"Don't you get it? We're through. You're fired."

Melanie stared at Mace, her eyes widening. "You're dumping me *now*? During the worst image crisis a 'naut's ever faced?"

"MELANIE!" Mace snapped. His knees gave out. He turned his back to the wall and crumpled to the floor, where he hugged his shins with his free arm. His hands were shaking. "Leave me alone. There's no coming back from this. I . . . I can't race anymore. I'm done. I'm done with you. I'm done with speed. I'm done with TURBO."

GAUNTLET WEEK

CHAPTER TEN //////

The airplane touched down on the runway in Punta Arenas, Chile. Now that the long flight was a thing of the past, Mace relaxed and breathed a sigh of relief.

The Patagonia region of South America was known for its long stretch of white-capped, jagged mountains lined with deep-blue glaciers. Mace had watched a movie on the flight about a Chilean soccer team whose plane had crashed on one of the mountains. The survivors had stayed alive by agreeing to eat the remains of those who had died.

Horrified, Mace had instantly regretted his selection of

onboard entertainment, but he couldn't peel his eyes away from the film. It had everything he loved in a good flick: sports, beautiful backdrops, high suspense, and zero Thaddeus Hightower.

Mace's ribs were still tender to the touch. He'd been stuffed in a coach window seat since departing Santiago five hours earlier, and before that, he'd sprinted through the airport to catch his final flight after a delayed red-eye arrival from Houston and further hang-ups at Chilean passport control. The customs officials had been suspicious of Mace's TURBO helmet (which contained a redundant back-up pressurized breathing apparatus for submersible and high-altitude terrains).

"I'm Mace Blazer," he'd told the customs official. "Renegade? I used to be a TURBOnaut."

The Chilean had stared at him impatiently. "I know who you were. Why do you need a helmet? Are you going to blow up the plane and skydive away?"

"What? No!" *I call it quits,* Mace lamented, *and now I'm a potential terrorist.* "I need my uniform for interviews. It's just for show."

Melanie used to arrange everything and make

emergencies disappear, but it had taken Mace enough time to sort out his passport and his special item permits during his layover in Santiago that he'd almost missed his connecting flight.

He deplaned and made his way to the baggage conveyor belt. While he waited, he felt a gentle tap on his shoulder. He turned. Aya stood behind him.

She was the only 'naut who'd beaten Hightower since the actor had entered the sport. She'd done it twice, both times early on. She'd taken first in the Great Lakes and then later gone on to squeak out a win in South Africa. But The Leading Man had become impossible to overtake as the season wore on.

Thad Hightower's utter dominance in the sport was by far the worst part of quitting for Mace. But it hadn't been enough to keep his stomach from turning into processed cheese goo whenever Mace even thought about getting near the cockpit of *Trailblazer*.

"Glad you made it," Aya told Mace. "You look a little better every time I see you. How was the trip?"

"I'm good," Mace summarized. "I almost missed the connection in Santiago, though."

"I mean, how'd you do on the flight?"

Mace felt his cheeks flush with mild embarrassment. "I really don't get anxious, as long as I'm not the one behind the wheel."

"How are your parents?" she asked. "I'm surprised they didn't join you."

Mace shrugged. "Well, I'm not racing. They're on a big retreat in the Rockies with the kids from their new school. I'm supposed to email them every couple days; otherwise it's an unplugged, no-electronics sort of retreat. I'm my own man for the week."

"That's cool," said Aya. "I'm glad they trust you."

Mace let out a rueful laugh. "Since everything happened, I think they're worried I'm too boring now."

"I'm pretty freed up too," Aya noted. "My folks are taking off after dinner tonight for some meetings in Brazil. But they'll be back to watch the Prix."

Looking around, Mace asked, "Is Dex here?"

Aya laughed. "You'll have to settle for me. They bumped his track time to now."

"How's he doing?"

"We don't talk much. I am the competition, after all.

But I know he's nervous. I think it's great that you made the effort to come. Since you're here, I'm sure he'll perk up."

"I'm happy to try. Guess I know a thing or two about being in a funk." Mace sighed.

Dex had qualified for the Gauntlet by the skin of his teeth, with a string of third-place showings intermixed with a slew of poorer performances. The rocky rollout to his solo career had taken a toll on his psyche, apparently. And Kreznia's struggle for independence, which was heating up in the news these days, wasn't helping matters. Olesya Vasko was Dex's biggest financial backer. But her father had suddenly redirected her TURBO funds toward other expenses.

Mace picked up his jumble of bags. A stab of pain flashed along his side, but it didn't last.

"Here, let me help." Mace knew there was no use arguing with Aya, so he let her grab a few of the bags. She hefted one of the duffels. "Wait, why'd you bring your helmet and suit? Keeping your options open, Mr. Boring?"

He shook his head. "It's for my *TURBOWORLD* interview."

One of Aya's eyebrows arched. "You're doing an interview?"

Mace hadn't spoken to the media since making his

abrupt exit from the sport. "I need to. To help pay for the trip. But . . . I think I'm ready to talk. I feel like I owe everyone an explanation of some kind."

Aya nodded. "I hope it goes well. It's good to see you coming around."

Mace offered a grim smile. "We'll see. I'm happy to be able to be here for you and Dex, at least."

They stepped out of the airport, and Mace immediately fished a coat from his luggage. He crossed his arms and shivered. It was cold! While it was late summer back home, the southern hemisphere was just emerging from winter. Gray piles of parking lot snow remained as evidence of a recent storm.

Aya pointed out a teenager wearing slick shades, holding up a strip of cardboard with Mace's name on it. "I've got crew coming on the next flight so I'm going to stay, but there's your ride into town." She handed him a green-and-purple lanyard and a keycard printed with his photo and a bar code. "This'll get you same access as my crew, anywhere you want to go. Use it to track down Dex once you get settled. I'm doing dinner with my parents and some sponsors tonight if you want to join."

"No, thanks. I've already had enough excitement today. I'll track you down tomorrow after my interview."

"Sounds good." Aya saluted. "Make every morph matter." She hurried back inside the warm airport.

Mace approached the young man with the sunglasses.

"Renegade!" the teenager said, vigorously shaking Mace's waiting hand. "It's a real honor. Welcome to Punta Arenas! Welcome to Tierra del Fuego. My name's Juan Pablo Garcia. I also go by JP."

"*Mucho gusto*, JP," Mace said.

"*Mucho gusto,*" Juan Pablo replied. "I'm here to show you around, get you anything you need. What do you want to do first?"

Mace grimaced. This guy seemed so enthusiastic. "I really just want to check in to my room and unpack. Is that okay?"

"Sure thing, *jefe*! No problem!" JP answered. "Like I said, whatever you need. I know it's a long way from *Los Estados* to the end of the world down here. Let's get you set. Freshen up, recharge, and I'll take you back out and show you around whenever you're up for it."

They walked to the parking lot as they talked. JP carried Mace's bags. "Your English is very good," Mace offered.

"Oh, thanks. I got around a lot as a kid. My parents ran some businesses in the States for a while."

He placed Mace's luggage in the back of a rather sweet-looking Mitsubishi Eclipse. "Nice wheels, man."

"Now I know you're just being nice. Crash a Mazagatti and you gawk at my Eclipse?" Mace winced at the mention of the accident. "Oh, my bad, man. I shouldn't've brought that up!"

Mace reached for a change of topic. "Your car's boss. Really. The nitrous oxide injection system . . . I hope that's not just for show."

"You're all right, Mace Blazer." JP smiled. "More torque to the wheels and faster acceleration. How'd you pick up on the engine mods so fast?"

Mace shrugged. "I just know machines."

JP opened the passenger door for Mace, made sure he was comfortable inside, and then walked around the Eclipse to take the driver's seat. "Hey, check this out. We're giving you the star treatment. Police escort."

JP pointed with pursed lips as he pulled out of the parking lot. A police cruiser fell in line in front of the Eclipse and turned on its flashing lights. "My uncle is the chief of police here," Juan Pablo explained. "He was happy to spare a deputy for you. My idea."

"Nice," Mace said. But he was uncomfortable. He didn't deserve so much respect. *You almost killed a baby. If anything, you should be in the back seat of a police cruiser, not behind one.*

They exited the airport and headed into town. JP drove quietly, and Mace took in the sights. Punta Arenas was coastal, marking the end of the South American continental land mass. The Pacific Ocean was visible almost everywhere along the road. But it wasn't open ocean. To the east and to the south lay Tierra del Fuego: one large island about the size of Louisiana, along with thousands of smaller mountainous islets. Half of Tierra del Fuego belonged to Chile and the other half to Argentina. The Prix would rocket in and out of both countries, in and out of hundreds of watery channels separating the tall islands, and up and down steep, snowbound slopes.

It would have been a fun race, he lamented inwardly.

"What's that?" Mace asked, pointing at a strange-looking

ship completely out of the water near a harbor. It was very fat, tall, and round, and oddly foreshortened. And it was made entirely of wood.

"Oh, that's a model of one of the original ships Magellan sailed when he was the first person to circumnavigate the world. His route took him right through this wide channel that separates the continent from the big islands farther south. The currents are dangerous down around Cape Horn, which is the very bottom tip of Tierra del Fuego, so ships mostly went through these channels when they passed between the Atlantic Ocean and the Pacific. The Prix'll go through here, too."

The town of Punta Arenas was colorful, with brightly painted homes and metal-roofed buildings laid out in a grid along coastal cliffs and windswept, grassy beaches. The air was clean, and visibility was what they referred to in the business as "infinite." Mace dug the vibe he was getting from the town and decided he could enjoy being here for the better part of a week, even if it was only to help snap his friend out of a rut.

JP gave the Eclipse a lot of gas on the open road, and he passed the cop car. No traffic in either direction. He reached for a switch on his center console. "Want to get a feel for the nox?" he asked his passenger playfully.

Mace grew cold and stiff. He shut his eyes, gripping his seat with balled-up fingers. He had no way of knowing how good a driver JP was. "Can you not . . . do that? Please?"

"Oh. Oh, sorry," JP answered, letting off the gas and falling back behind their escort.

Mace reopened his eyes and reminded himself to breathe. He caught JP's concerned expression and felt embarrassed.

"I wasn't thinking, *jefe*. Sorry. I didn't know it was so . . ." JP abandoned his observation in mid-sentence. Whatever he was going to say—bad? serious?—only made the situation more awkward.

"Some TURBOnaut I am, eh?" Mace offered.

"Hey, it's cool. I get it."

Mace nodded, but he didn't think JP had any clue what Mace was going through. Not really.

That mother was pushing a BABY STROLLER.

"Mind if I ask you something?" JP probed.

Mace sighed. "Go ahead. Everyone does."

"All right," JP said. "You'll be back for next season, yeah?"

"We'll see." Mace said. But he knew the answer was no.

"You've gotta take on Hightower. He's so obnoxious. You gotta take him down."

Mace shook his head. "Someone does. But it won't be me. I'm just helping out on TURBOWORLD for now. And being there for my friends."

"I had a scary race earlier this year," JP said. "Shook me up good. Bad crash, but it was the other guy, not me. Even so, I totally got a feeling for how it messes with you. It was when you won in the Alps. I was street racing—against a tri-morpher."

"Really?" Mace said. "Hobby leaguer?"

"No. Like, state-of-the-art stuff. Guy totally biffed it, though."

Mace held his tongue. This story didn't make any sense. An owner of a real morpher wouldn't risk damage to such a machine by racing a kid in the streets. But he didn't say anything. He liked JP and didn't want to offend him.

But then again, if Mace was idiotic enough to smash up a Maz and nearly kill a *baby*, maybe other world-class idiots populated the earth here and there, too.

"You should see what I'm talking about. Want to? It'll only take a minute."

"I don't know." Mace rolled his eyes. He just wanted to get unpacked and track down Dex.

"Come on," JP coaxed. "Seriously, I think it's right up your alley."

This guy was being so nice. Mace figured he owed him a spare moment. "Okay. Let's check it out."

JP called the escort in front of them, and they veered off course toward the cliffs overlooking the channel.

A minute later, Mace was at full attention.

He stood beside JP and the deputy along the edge of the high bluff, looking down at a boulder pile tormented by the powerful waves.

"See the frame there? What's left of it?"

"I do," Mace said, his eyes glued to the burnt and twisted wreckage. "And you're certain that was a morpher?"

"It sprouted wings. Gorgeous, too. I haven't seen a racer like it before or since."

"And you never met the driver?" Mace pressed.

"No. He just vanished. But it was full dark. And we never

found a seat in the wreckage, not even a burnt skeleton of one. So they ejected somewhere."

He wanted a closer look. "Can I go down there?"

JP asked the deputy something in Spanish then turned to Mace and nodded. "He's got a rope in his trunk. We'll tie it around you and lower you down if you want."

Mace wasn't sure how his recovering spleen and gallbladder and ribs would feel about that, but he couldn't resist.

A few minutes later, Mace had his coat off, and the Chileans were ready to lower him over the cliff's edge. The rope was tied securely around his upper chest, and they began to let out some slack along the bumper pulley system they'd constructed. "Don't take too long," JP told him. "Tide's coming in. Seriously, watch for rogue waves."

Mace offered his assistants a thumbs-up, already wincing from the pain. He had rappelled before, during a weekend eco-adventure ahead of his race in the Alps, but that had involved expensive, technical equipment. This homemade getup was uncomfortable and scary. And he was shivering from the cold. Nonetheless, Mace got a rhythm going, kicking off the cliff wall as his belayers let out more rope, and he touched down on the slippery rocks without a hitch.

He unlooped himself from the dangling rope and struggled on uncertain feet to scramble over to where the wreckage was. His chest hurt, but his healed broken arm gave him no discomfort at all. He noted with a stab of regret: physically, he definitely would've been Prix-ready this week.

When he reached the hunks of debris, he had to time his investigation with the ebb and flow of the waves, darting in and out every several seconds. He felt like a shorebird. But he was glad he'd bothered to come down here. There was a lot he was learning from this mystery wreckage, more than JP and his uncle could have known.

For one, he knew immediately that this had indeed been a trimorpher. He'd been skeptical of the fact up until this moment, but charred-out transformer modules peppered the rocks in and around the chassis. And what was left of the engine was a dual turbine/rocket design. He couldn't identify the brand—the fire had been hot enough to fuse metal parts together and melt away distinguishing features.

Mace also confirmed that an ejector seat had been launched. The ejector clamps on the floor were locked open, and JP was right—there was no hint of a seat anywhere.

The pilot of this craft was just as likely to have died at sea upon ejecting as they were to have landed safely in the dark somewhere. It was impossible to tell.

"Weird," he said under his breath, confessing his intrigue to the waves. He had noticed the quality of the design and the materials and components that went into this trimorpher. He knew from the photos on JP's phone that it was cutting-edge, some kind of prototype. It had been a lavish specimen of advanced engineering and design. For someone to pit it against a local teenager—it didn't add up.

There was only one person he could think of who was rich enough to toss around trimorphers like paper airplanes.

"Tempest Hollande."

He glanced south toward the tall island mountains of Tierra del Fuego, as if scanning the skies for her return. *She's dead,* he scolded himself. But he wasn't convinced—he never had been. In his heart he believed she was still out there somewhere, planning something.

"I'll be watching for you," he promised the end of the world. "And whatever you're up to, I'll be ready."

CHAPTER ELEVEN //////

The phone rang.

Finally! Mace jumped up from his hotel bed and snatched his cell. "Hello!"

"Mace, hi."

It was Olesya Vasko. At last, he was getting somewhere. He muted the volume on the Chilean TV show he'd been watching, a Spanish-language news program that was showing images, of all things, of the princess's father storming angrily out of a meeting somewhere in eastern Europe. The word *Kreznia* had been coming up a lot, but he couldn't make heads or tails of what was going on. "Thanks for calling me back. I've been looking everywhere for you."

"I was in the air. You just missed me. I'm in Montevideo for the night, but I'll be back your way tomorrow evening."

"I'm watching your dad on the TV right now," Mace admitted. "He looks mad."

"Yeah, things aren't going well. We've got troops showing up on our doorstep. We're not surprised, though. It's all under control."

Mace remembered Dex's frustration with how things were turning out. "It's not distracting you from the Prix?"

"War games are my dad's thing. I told Dex: once I get back, I'm 100 percent focused on the Glove! I'm TURBO all the way. Which is why I'm calling you back. They said it was urgent. I'm hoping it's about you taking your spot in the lineup. I'll fly right back if that's what you need my help with."

"No—no, it's not," Mace stammered, momentarily flummoxed. It wasn't just what she was saying, it was how she was saying it. Her voice was commanding, but in the warmest possible way. He had forgotten her confidence and charisma. "I'm looking for Dex, actually. We . . . I can't get ahold of him. I know he's been freaking out about the race, and I wanted to talk to him."

"Sorry, I don't know where he is," Olesya said. "Ask his crew chief."

"I did. I went to the team garage, but they told me to scram. They said Dex isn't interested in seeing anybody right now."

"That doesn't make a lot of sense," said the princess. "Dex would take your call, right?"

"I don't know what the crew told him," said Mace. "But then I got ahold of his sister back in the DR. She said Dex texted her asking her to leave him alone before the race. Both of us agreed that didn't sound like him. Do you know where he's staying? Maybe if I camp out, I can catch him. Did you know he missed his time on the track this afternoon?"

"He did?" The princess was surprised by this. "That's weird. I'll check in with the crew myself."

"If something's wrong, you need to tell me," Mace insisted. A warning bell was going off in his head.

"Nothing's wrong, Mace. But I'll get to the bottom of it and get back to you. Just do me a favor, meanwhile. Will you? Please, Mace: suit up. You need to show Hightower what you can do."

"Olesya," Mace said pointedly. "I'm here for Dex. That's all."

She sighed heavily over the phone, exasperated. "That's too bad. But I will check in with you. Okay? *Mañana en la mañana.*"

She hung up. Mace held the phone in his hand for a minute, totally baffled. *What's my next move?* he wondered. He looked at the time. It was already nine p.m. He'd lost his entire afternoon and evening. Something wasn't right.

He called Aya, who answered right away. "You find him?"

"No." Mace rubbed the back of his neck. "I don't like it. Dex wouldn't avoid us like this, no matter how nervous he is."

"I know," agreed Aya. "And we can't go to the Association without risking revealing his identity. And I don't feel like snooping around Punta Arenas after dark. What do you want to do?"

"I'm tied up on the *TURBOWORLD* set first thing tomorrow. They'll throw a fit if I bail." Silence held the line for a moment, and then Mace thought of something. "Hey, what if we ask that JP guy to look into things? His uncle's in charge of the local police."

"Good idea!" answered Aya. "If they come up with any-thing, I'll let you know first thing in the morning."

"Sounds good." Mace released a pent-up breath. "If they don't track him down, though . . ." His stomach did a flip.

"But he'll turn up," Aya reassured him. "We're just get-ting ahead of ourselves."

"Oh, I know. I'm sure he's fine." Mace was quick to agree. "It is weird, but we'll figure it out."

/////// CHAPTER TWELVE

The studio tech finished adjusting the mic on Mace's flight suit, straightened the collar, and stepped out of the shot. "Let's check your levels as the trimorpher comes around," he said.

Mace interlaced his fingers, resting his hands on the glass desktop, looked into the camera, and spoke in a normal volume. "How much wood would a woodchuck chuck?" His voice was drowned out in his own ears as *I'd Like to Thank the Academy* bulleted by, the roar of its pounding pistons filling the air.

"Audio's good. It's loud out here, but don't raise your voice. The audiences will hear you fine." The tech gave the cast and crew a thumbs-up and darted for the control booth.

Mace glanced behind himself at the stretch of stadium asphalt and the empty grandstands beyond. He was a guest on today's production of *TURBOWORLD*, and he and Jax Anders would be broadcasting live all morning, on location, from the center of the raceway. He wore his *Trailblazer* flight suit. All part of the theatrics of being on camera. But he had enjoyed slipping into his old uniform. It was a cozy outfit for this weather, and he missed the feel of its flexible, breathable fabric against his skin.

The track was in use every daylight hour, as Prix rivals calibrated their machines to race smoothly in the region's cold, wet, and windy weather. Any second now *I'd Like to Thank the Academy* and The Leading Man would scream by at top speed, completing another lap of Hightower's endurance trial.

Mace didn't want to be forced to watch The Leading Man's flawless execution. But as long as Hightower was on the test track, they couldn't accidentally run into each other, so Mace chalked the situation up as a win.

"You're looking well," Jax Anders told him from across the glass surface of his iconic sportscaster desk. He wore a bright windbreaker over a suit and tie and giant red-white-and-blue earmuffs. "It's good to see you back in the thick of it."

"Thanks," Mace said. "Still pretty stiff," he added.

It *was* nice to be in the thick of it, Mace noted. He had worried that simply being around so many trimorphers would make him visibly anxious. But as Hightower zoomed around the track again, he scarcely flinched.

"Jax, we're live in ten, nine . . . ," the set director declared from the shadows. He counted down silently with his fingers. On the studio cameras, a green light blinked.

Mace's phone rang. It was Aya. He took the call, in spite of the set director's evil glare.

"We're live any second. What's up?"

"I think I have a lead. Dex might actually be in trouble."

"Wait. What?"

"Can we talk in person? I'm at the garages."

"Right now? I can't. We're going on air."

Aya was out of breath, talking fast. "JP says he saw Princess Vasko with *Hightower*. This morning."

"No way." Mace wasn't in disbelief. He was certain this was a mistake. "JP's confused. The princess is in Montevideo."

"MACE!" shouted the set director. "We're live in two . . . one . . ."

Aya grunted. "I know. It's not adding up. But I'm following up now. Meet me at the hangars as soon as you can."

Mace severed the call and shoved the phone in his flight suit chest pocket, springing to attention. The flashing green lights turned solid.

Anders spoke into his camera, his posture upright, his chin level. His breath was visible coming out of his mouth. "Welcome back, maniacs, to *TURBOWORLD*'s station on location. We're coming to you live from Punta Arenas, Chile, in the heart of Patagonia, the gateway to Tierra del Fuego and the site of this year's eminent and imminent Gauntlet Prix. Welcome to Magellan Raceway, host of both the green flag *and* the checkered flag. Three days till launch, the world's greatest sporting extravaganza has descended en masse upon the majestic and tranquil ocean-skirted mountains at the bottom of the world. We have Mace Blazer, Renegade himself, in the studio today, and we're all dying to know what his plans are. Later, we'll bring you an update on the Prix's impact on breeding southern right whale populations due to invasive algae blooms. The league is requiring chemical sanitizing baths for the vehicles. Stay tuned, maniacs. We'll be right back with the interview you've all been waiting for."

"And . . . cut," said the studio director. "Short station ID break. Stay ready."

A small television under the glass table played a commercial with closed captioning. It was there to show Anders and his guests what audiences at home were seeing. "*TURBO-WORLD* is brought to you by Infinite Dynamic," read the display. On the screen, a satellite orbited high above the Earth. The planet morphed into a biological cell, and the satellite transformed into a nanobot, infiltrating it. "Tomorrow's intelligence. Applied today."

A makeup lady darted in and dabbed Mace's forehead. "Sweating in this cold?"

"Dex might actually be in trouble."

His mind had been racing during Anders's preamble. Hightower and Vasko together? This morning? It must be a mistake. But even if it were true, what did it prove? What did it mean? So what if Dex's sponsor was seen with Hightower?

Vasko was probably just fangirling him. But then why was she back in Punta Arenas so early? Had she lied to Mace about being gone? Why would she do that?

The loud purr of a trimorpher approached from behind at high speed, then slowed rapidly. Mace watched on the small television monitor as *I'd Like to Thank the Academy* pulled up and parked in the grass behind himself and the anchor. Black smoke rose in a sustained curtain through the seams along *Academy*'s hood.

Hightower climbed out of the cockpit. He pulled off his helmet and immediately put on his golden mirror-surface aviator sunglasses. He leaned against his roadster, arms crossed, staring morosely at the smoke. The emergency crew scurried over, but he ordered the responders to leave his vehicle alone.

"Just let it cool off," Mace heard him instruct. "I'll get it back to the warehouse and deal with it there."

Mace hid a frown as he watched all this unfold. High-tower exhibited zero respect for *I'd Like to Thank the Academy*. When he'd arrived for his track time this morn-ing, he had appeared out of nowhere and had jumped right in his golden trimorpher. TURBOnauts weren't prone to ignoring their rides, though. Mace knew from his own experience and from watching others: 'nauts arrived early, personally conducted walk-throughs and checked off checklist items, spoke at length with their crew chiefs, peered under the hood, and inspected their transformer modules, tires, fins, engines, and other components. They oversaw diagnostic tests and stroked their trimorphers' hulls affectionately. An undisputable relationship existed between 'nauts, their steeds, and their crew at large. But Mace had never witnessed Thaddeus acting the part of the jockey to a thoroughbred horse.

The studio guy growled. "Look at your camera, Mace!" He dialed into his surroundings. The green lights were solid again.

"Welcome back, maniacs." Anders was in his own world, which consisted of just him and several million viewers at home around the globe. "Here with us right now: Mace Blazer. So, let's start with the question everyone's asking. Are you going to race for the Glove, Renegade? You qualified for a slot a long time ago. You had a stellar season opening. And everyone wants to see what you can do against Hollywood's—and TURBO racing's—Leading Man. Do you have any news to share with us today?"

He forced a short laugh. "No announcements. I'll tell you: it's fun to be back in this suit. But I'm not ready to be back in the saddle. I'm just not."

"You're not the first crash survivor I've interviewed," Jax revealed. "It's usually a traumatic experience. But 'nauts do recover and sometimes come screaming back. But not you?"

The TV set positioned beneath the glass desk showed Mace what audiences were seeing. He looked exactly the way he felt: small, washed up. Remorseful. He forced himself to meet the interviewer's eyes and slowly nodded. "The crash shook me up, for sure. But it was the complete lapse in judgment on my part that haunts me. I put others in danger in London, not just myself. Until I can trust myself again, I can't get back on the track."

"Understandable, I suppose. Respectable, even. But I don't think I'm only speaking for myself when I say I'm disappointed to hear that," Jax Anders admitted, tapping a pen on the desk. "You know, last year's Prix counted, but there'll always be an asterisk next to your name, Renegade."

"Huh?"

"You know what I'm talking about: the Caribbean

hypercane reduced the competition to one day, and several other pilots had to bow out along the route due to complications of the storm. I was hoping you could give your fans what you owe them this go-around: a straight-up, throw down, flat-out win."

Mace frowned. "But this year's Prix is only one day, too," he argued.

Anders nodded. "A Prix can be variable in length, depending on location. There aren't enough population centers in this region—and too many environmental restrictions—to justify a two-stage Prix this year. But that was decided and agreed upon a while back. Your victory last year involved a sudden surprise adjustment that rattled everyone."

Mace was thrown by the point Jax Anders was making.

There'll always be an asterisk next to your name, Renegade. . . .

But his uneasiness wasn't enough to change the fact that he simply wasn't ready to compete again.

Mace shrugged unhelpfully on camera. "I don't even have *Trailblazer* down here with me. So I don't know what you're hoping for."

Thaddeus Hightower popped up onstage, grabbed a seat,

and wheeled it over to the anchor table. He wore a bright, happy grin.

Jax Anders was a hard man to render speechless, but he was caught completely off guard by Hightower's surprise appearance. "Yo, Jax, you going to mic me up so Blazer and I can chat, or are you going to keep staring at me with your mouth open like a fish waiting for a hook?"

Mace braced himself, secretly flustered. *Keep your cool.*

Jax jolted back to life. "Hey, this is great!" he said. "Get him a mic!"

A tech hurriedly pinned a mic to Hightower's golden flight suit and scurried off camera. "Trouble under the hood?" Anders asked.

Hightower waved off his concern. "Oh, something blew in there. We'll get it patched up. Business as usual at my speeds. But I was standing there and glanced over, and I thought to myself, is that Mace Blazer?" He held out his hand to Mace. "Nice to see you suited up. Does this mean what I think it means? I hope it does!"

Mace reluctantly accepted the handshake and offered a muted, "Hi."

"We were just talking about you," Jax explained. "Mace

was coming straight from the heart. Sounds like he has some more soul-searching to do before the two of you square off."

Hightower sighed explosively. "Well, that's typical. I suppose it's probably a wise decision."

Mace gritted his teeth, forced a smile, and attempted a casual reply. "I let my fans down. I understand I have to earn their trust again. That takes time."

"The terrain's the best place to earn respect."

Mace rolled his eyes, realizing too late the cameras would have broadcast his reaction for the whole world to see. For some reason, this made him laugh. The Leading Man was not amused. This only made Mace laugh again, harder. He'd dug himself a deep hole now. But he didn't care. He was starting to feel free. It was nice just to be himself on camera for a change.

"You're dismissing him?" asked Anders, matching Renegade's playful smile.

"Jax, it's okay," said Mace. "Rad Thad is young. Maybe he'll get his priorities straight once he matures."

Someone on the studio crew audibly oohed.

"Why won't you race me, Blazer?" Hightower interjected.

He pressed his palms down on the table and leaned in toward the others as he talked. "You know you can't beat me, that's why. No one can. I'm the best this sport's ever seen!"

The studio fell silent. All eyes were on Hightower, who seemed to realize he'd been ranting. He straightened up, his toothy grin taking over his face.

"That's quite a claim you're making," Anders pointed out.

"Why shouldn't I make it? Who can prove me wrong?" he explained confidently. He pointed a thumb over his shoulder at his trimorpher, which was no longer smoking. "We're shaving seconds off our record lap times. I'm still improving out there. It's getting lonely at the front of the pack. Don't be a coward, Mace Blazer. Get back in your trimorpher and race me. That's all I have left to say."

"Thad"—Mace offered him a saccharine smile—"were you with Olesya Vasko this morning?"

"What?" Hightower snapped. "What's that got to do with anything?"

Mace jolted. "So, you were?"

The actor froze. "No. I wasn't with anyone."

"What are you talking about, Mace?" pressed Jax.

Mace almost blurted everything out to the sportscaster. *Caballero's gone missing! And Thad was seen with his biggest sponsor!* But his mouth hung open and no words came forth.

We're still on camera. . . .

Hightower would deny all of it. And Mace didn't know anything for sure. What was he accusing Hightower of, anyway? Kidnapping? Because Aya told him over the phone that JP told her over the phone that he'd seen the actor and the princess in the same room at the same time?

Mace didn't know any of the details. All he knew for sure was that his friend was missing, and Dex's crew seemed to be covering for the fact. His heartbeat quickened.

He shrugged innocently for effect. "I mean . . . I just know she's a fan."

"That Kreznian royal?" Thad scratched the back of his head, pretending to think. "She sure is. She wanted an autograph. What, you want one too?"

"Coming up on the weather report," chimed the set director.

Anders grunted. "And with that, we'll be right back, maniacs. Lots to think about and lots still to come. Stay tuned for more Mace Blazer, right after the impeccable Paulie Meckel gives us our latest race-day weather rundown."

"And we're off air!" the set director announced.

"Why are you even talking to him?" Hightower asked Anders. "He's yesterday's news. He's done. He's washed up. His career is over, and everyone knows it." The actor jumped angrily off the stage and stormed toward his roadster.

I'd Like to Thank the Academy took to the track, trailing tendrils of smoke. Mace watched the trimorpher sputter away, baffled.

"What was all that about?" Jax probed.

"I know. I'm sorry," Mace admitted. "I was just . . . trying to get under his skin."

"Looks like it worked," Jax said. "Movie stars can be so weird."

You should tell him Caballero has disappeared, Mace thought. *Let the press help track him down.*

But then Mace's phone vibrated. He stole a quick glance at the screen, finding a text from Aya:

Dex's crew chief just flew off in his morpher. I'm following in Lotus. Heading south. May go out of range but I'll text update ASAP.

"What the heck?" he said aloud.

"Something wrong?" Jax asked.

Something is definitely not right.

Mace shoved the phone in his pocket. "Hey, Jax? I'm sorry. I've gotta go." He unclipped his mic and stood up.

"What is it now?" barked the set director. "This isn't a game of Whac-A-Mole!"

"Mace, you can't just leave," Jax warned him, incredulous. "We have you scheduled all morning."

"I'm sorry," Mace reiterated. He jumped off the dais and darted away toward the stadium exits.

The green light blinked on. Jax's head whipped back to the camera and he automatically started talking. "Aaaand, once again, we're back, maniacs!" He was suddenly alone at his glass desk, droning on, unaware that the biggest scoop in the history of TURBO was unfolding in front of his nose.

CHAPTER THIRTEEN //////

Light snow fell off and on amid occasional frigid wind gusts. The snow wasn't sticking, but the walkway was icy. Mace texted Aya twice during his slow jog between the raceway and the trimorpher storage bays, asking her to check in again.

She never responded.

Mace picked up his pace, although he wasn't really sure what good it would do.

With a simple swipe of his Team Katana keycard, he slipped into the facility and set off into the large warehouse toward *Lotus*'s stall. Maybe someone from her crew could fill him in.

He passed Dex's hangar. The garage was locked shut. He placed an ear against the bay door and listened. Within, all was quiet and still. He felt certain *Silverado* wasn't inside. But where had the crew chief taken it? Mace's worry for Aya's safety notched up. Again, he checked his phone for an update from her. Nothing.

He hurried down the hallway. Before reaching the Katana team stall, he came across *Academy*'s garage. The Leading Man's trimorpher was backed into its parking spot. Faint hints of smoke still rose from the hood. Hightower was still inside the cockpit, visible as a moving silhouette. Mace crouched behind a waist-high concrete wall, wondering what to do.

He was about to move on toward *Lotus*'s hangar, but his eyes snagged on an item resting off-kilter atop a tool chest: a black cowboy hat.

That belongs to Dex. Mace was sure of it.

But then he wasn't so sure. *There's more than one black cowboy hat in the world*, he cautioned himself. He needed a closer look.

The dark canopy of *Academy* lifted. Hightower climbed out, removed his helmet, and plugged a thick diagnostics cable into the hull. He spent a moment rummaging through items on a workbench before emerging from the garage. He punched in a security code on the stall's garage door and marched off toward the stairwell leading to the upper-level office suites. After several warning beeps, the door to the stall began to lower.

Now's your chance! Mace had no time to second-guess himself. He vaulted the low wall, scurried across the cavern-ous warehouse, and used his slick flight suit to slide feet-first under the closing door.

The door slammed against the polished concrete floor. The room's interior lights clicked off. Mace sat up slowly, careful not to make a sound.

His eyes adjusted to the dim lighting provided only by the vehicle's display panels. Equipment lined the benches along the walls. Nothing stirred. Mace took to his feet and moved through the dark over to the cowboy hat.

This could definitely be his, he decided, inspecting it with his fingers and holding it close. But if he was going to go to the police, claiming that Thad Hightower had had something to do with Dex's disappearance, he needed to be certain.

Mace used the light of his phone to check the hat's label. Maybe Dex had written his name or initials somewhere. But no such luck.

What else is here?

He placed the hat back on the drawer of tools and approached *I'd Like to Thank the Academy.* Its glass canopy was propped fully open. Mace did a double take, his eyes slowly widening. There was a large empty space behind the seat. That's where the crash foam and airbags and the compressor systems for both should be stored. But the essential safety features were entirely absent from the vehicle!

Other than an ejector seat, *Academy* had no collision protection. Thaddeus Hightower could easily be smashed to mush if he ever had an accident on the terrain . . . especially in a midair collision! The safety system must've been removed to make his morpher lighter. But Hightower had only been running time trials today. Setting new lap records during a training run with zero safety equipment was as stupid as it was insane.

A latch snapped somewhere, and the sound cracked through the room like a whip. It was followed by the unmistakable rumble of something sliding open. *The door! He's back already!* Mace bolted for cover. But the garage door remained sealed. So where was the sound coming from? He placed a hand on the ground and felt the source of the grinding. He looked up. A vent on the ceiling had opened, accompanied by an eerie red light emanating from somewhere high up the shaft. An automated voice pierced the room. "Decontamination commencing."

"Oh no," Mace cried. He knew what this was. *I'd Like to Thank the Academy* was about to get a chemical bath. It was standard procedure after submarine runs here, to keep the environmentalists happy. The chemical rinse process was intended to make sure no hint of invasive algae hitchhiked on the trimorphers.

The chemicals were deadly to all biological organisms—which happened to include both invasive algae and Mace Blazer.

He tried to open the garage door, but it had auto-locked for the process.

I'm trapped!

Smoke poured out of the vent, lit by a menacing red glow. Mace backed away. Thank God he was in his flight suit, which protected all his skin . . . except for his head.

My helmet's in the hotel, he realized.

With mounting panic, he scanned the room. Where had Hightower put his helmet? There was a cabinet against the far wall, the door ajar. He raced over, careful to hug the walls. Toxic smoke poured heavily down from the center of the ceiling, billowing out to fill the room once it struck the vehicle and the floor. Mace could make out the edges of the plume. He raised the neck bib of his flight suit to cover his face and nose as he cut through the expanding red-tinged mist. His eyes stung.

The cabinet had two helmets. Mace almost gasped his relief, but he knew he needed to keep holding his breath. He grabbed the nearest helmet. It was properly equipped with a regulator. He jammed it on his head, cinching it tight. He grabbed a towel from the nearby workbench and wrapped it around his neck, then crouched in the corner. The room had fogged over fully, like a sauna. He couldn't hold his breath any longer. His chest betrayed him, drawing in a lungful of air.

The air tasted and smelled clean. He let his breath back out heavily, propping the front of his visor against a trembling hand.

That had been close.

"Stupid algae," he said into the visor.

The decontamination process lasted a couple minutes. Mace waited it out as he gathered his nerves. Then a powerful vacuum sound commenced. The smoke retreated into the vent. The room was visibly free of mist, but the vacuum continued, and Mace waited. Finally, the red light switched to green, and the vent slammed shut.

"Decontamination complete. Air quality levels within normal parameters."

Mace sat huddled in the corner for another two minutes, just to be sure. Hesitantly, he loosened the towel and then the mask's chin strap. He pulled both away, testing the air. He could detect nothing wrong.

Except that when he glanced down at the helmet, he saw that it belonged to Dex.

///// CHAPTER FOURTEEN

Mace's breathing quickened. "Dex," he said, knowing for certain now that his worst fears for his friend were proving true. The helmet was black and silver, with spurs and a lasso in the design. It undeniably belonged to Caballero, and it had absolutely no business in a cabinet in Hightower's garage.

He jumped to his feet, his head full of new questions. *Is he taking out his competition?* A stab of fear rifled through him. "What'd you do with him?" he asked the air. "He better be safe."

I have proof, he realized. *I have to get this to the police.*

He clutched his friend's helmet and stood at the closed garage door, suddenly stymied. *How do I get out of here?* The locks were engaged, and they were electronic. He was sealed in. He would have to slip out once Thad or someone else returned.

He crouched behind a workbench and waited.

Several minutes passed. Mace stared at *I'd Like to Thank the Academy*, dimly lit in the mostly dark room. He thought of commandeering it—driving away in it as soon as the garage door opened—but decided it would be overkill and might complicate his argument of foul play on Hightower's part to the authorities. Besides, that thing was a death trap without its safety equipment. Not to mention the thought of getting behind the wheel again made his stomach twist.

As he waited, he started to wonder: why was *Academy* missing vital safety equipment?

He approached the open canopy, clutching Dex's helmet close. He leaned forward and studied the interior of the cockpit. The displays announced the ongoing progress of the diagnostic run-throughs, and Mace wasn't surprised to see the words *ENGINE COMPONENT DAMAGE CODE 8523—REPLACEMENT REQUIRED* flashing across the monitors. *That would explain the black smoke.* He didn't have diagnostic engine codes memorized, but the eight-thousand range consisted of critical functions.

He used his phone to snap a couple pictures of the empty area behind the seat. An unfamiliar metal casing and a panel of diodes took up some of the free space behind the seat, with fiber-optic wiring running up past the seat along the cabin wall toward the pedal well. *Weird.* He'd never seen anything like it. Teams often used custom tech under their hoods, but given *Academy*'s other oddities, Mace couldn't resist a closer inspection. He placed Dex's helmet on the seat and dove headfirst into the cockpit. He slipped his head as far as he could down under the steering wheel. The wiring ran farther back still. He wiggled down into the well of the seat so that his head was jammed between the pedals, and he used the light of his phone to get a closer look at the wiring running from the console over to the firewall.

Etched onto the narrow metal frame of a server bank was the name and logo of a company he couldn't place but felt like he should know.

Infinite Dynamic.

It took him a moment to connect the dots: Infinite

Dynamic was a big sponsor of *TURBOWORLD*. They made satellites and nanobots.

What the hell was their hardware doing behind the wheel of *I'd Like to Thank the Academy*?

The garage bay door lurched awake, rising. *Crap!*

The lights came on. Mace heard footsteps echoing nearer.

He tried to push himself out of the cockpit, but he was too crammed in to his upside-down position.

If Hightower spotted him in *Academy*'s cockpit—

If he caught Mace with Dex's helmet—

Mace couldn't afford to be found this way. He lifted an arm up and craned it around to reach the lower dash. Instinctively, he stabbed at the place he guessed the canopy switch would be. He was spot-on. The glass lid of the roadster lowered shut.

Just in time, it sealed. Good thing *Academy*'s glass was so darkly tinted.

Mace tucked himself into a ball and inched his way out from under the steering wheel into the driver's seat. With nowhere else to put it, he slipped Dex's helmet on his head.

Hightower circled the vehicle, cup of coffee in hand. He

paused to study a computer screen. Mace was petrified. What could he do? He was trapped, and the second the canopy lifted, he'd be cornered by Hightower himself. Thad would take back Caballero's helmet. He might even go make up a story about how he caught Mace trying to sabotage his craft.

Frozen in the seat, Mace watched helplessly as Hightower placed a palm along the security pad that would open the canopy.

The vehicle hissed, and the lid began to rise.

Mace remembered the empty crawlspace. With no other option, he slithered headfirst over the seat back and down through the tight squeeze behind it. He gathered up his legs and tucked in his knees.

He had a narrow view of Thaddeus Hightower looming over him, sipping the contents of a disposable coffee cup. The actor reached over to the dash controls with his free hand and tapped on something.

"I'm back," he told the displays.

A stranger's voice answered over the comm. "We're reading a faulty actuator under the hood, Thad. It only affects the roadster morph, but we're going to have to replace it at headquarters. Go ahead and come along for the ride. Join us back here."

"What? No can do," Hightower complained. "I have a spa treatment."

"We're overdue for a chat, anyway. Your outburst on *TURBOWORLD* isn't doing us any favors. Get down here. That's nonnegotiable." The voice coming from the radio speaker was male, older, and sounded American.

"Argh. Fine," Hightower pouted. "Now?"

"Let's get it out of the way. See you in a bit."

Hightower cursed and slapped the dash, killing the transmission. He wasted no time hopping up into the cockpit while balancing his coffee.

While Hightower sank into his smart cushioning, the canopy started to lower.

Mace clenched his jaw. He was stuck now. Revealing himself to Hightower was not an option. If he stayed quiet and still, Hightower might just be neglectful enough to never notice him. He might find a way to sneak away from this and get Dex's evidence in the right hands after all. Maybe he'd learn more along the way.

The engine came to life, releasing a belch of smoke.

Mace knew the feel of machines like no one else. He could tell something was wrong under the hood, but Hightower should be okay as long as he kept to normal speeds.

When the roadster lurched into gear, Mace took advantage of the bumpiness, squirming to sit himself up behind the pilot.

Academy left the warehouse and drove past the raceway through light snowfall. Mace was surprised when they merged onto the road leading into Punta Arenas. He'd taken for granted that "headquarters" would be close, but *Academy* suddenly accelerated and morphed to air, taking to the skies at a heavy angle.

No, no, no.

Mace battled a surge of panic. *I'm in a rocket. Sky high. And the safety systems have been replaced by* me.

He took several deep, controlled breaths. "Easy," he whispered. *Hightower is the best 'naut out there. Everything's going to be okay.*

The anxiety began to subside. Mace refused to let the terror in the back of his mind surface.

He made himself look out the canopy, where barren snowy ridgelines scrolled by. *I've got this*, he decided, and forced his nerves and muscles to relax.

But . . . were they going to be airborne for more than a few minutes? Mace wasn't sure he could hold still for much longer. His muscles were cramping up in this awkward, tight space.

It can't be that far, Mace convinced himself. Maybe Ushuaia—Argentina's southernmost city of respectable size. The Prix would pass through there. Made sense that Hightower's crew would have a replacement engine on hand at the team's staging booth. He could sneak away there, then get his evidence to the authorities.

Half an hour. I can do it, he convinced himself.

And that's when he overheard Hightower groan and stretch, muttering to himself, "What a drag. Can't stand Antarctica this time of year."

///// CHAPTER FIFTEEN

Anta-friggin'-WHAT?

Mace adjusted his weight, searching for a way to unscrunch his legs without brushing the seat back with his knees. His right foot was already falling asleep.

He searched his mind. How far away was Antarctica?

Mace knew the answer. *It's too far to fly without refueling.*

He had explored Antarctica on the map while studying this year's Prix route, drawn to the formidable, white expanse stretching away beneath where the action would take place. A long island chain extended its way north from the continent's main landmass, as if reaching out a tentacle to touch the tip of South America. In fact, the Andes and the Antarctic archipelago were part of the same mountain chain. The stretch of ocean between the continents was long and rough. Mace had read up on the Drake Passage—the weather patterns often generated hurricane-strength winds and thirty-to-fifty-foot waves.

He patted his chest pockets and fished his phone out. Still nothing from Aya. He needed to text JP, his parents, Gimbal—anyone and everyone—while he still could. But he had zero bars of service. It was already too late for him to alert anyone.

Mace heard slurping, then a satisfied, "Ahh." Then Hightower tossed his empty coffee cup over his shoulder. It bounced off Mace and fell away.

"You're joking," Mace growled to himself. Thaddeus was using the empty compartment behind the seat—which should have been filled with safety equipment—for *loose trash*?

He has no respect for this vehicle. Why do they make such a good team?

Mace watched the last evidence of land retreat behind

him. Steep cliffs, wracked by waves, faded into a haze of blue. Ahead: nothing but ocean and occasional clouds. So it was true. Their final destination was farther . . . south.

WHAT ABOUT OUR FUEL? Mace closed his eyes and battled back a wave of panic.

A movie started playing through the onboard speakers. Mace listened to familiar theme music, until he couldn't stand it any longer. *Why is he listening to a soundtrack? He needs to be able to hear the vehicle. We're heading into one of the worst weather patterns on the planet, and we don't even have enough FUEL.*

He risked stretching tall enough to see over the seat back and was rewarded with a truly bizarre sight.

Hightower wasn't listening to a movie soundtrack. He was watching a whole movie. The opening credits were almost over. It played on all dash and overhead displays simultaneously. And Mace was finally able to identify the music. It was from a terrible comedy called *Blind Allie*. Starring none other than Thaddeus Hightower himself.

"Oh my God, he's watching his own movie as onboard entertainment," Mace quietly told the air—which was growing noticeably colder by the minute.

A strong gust of wind slammed into *I'd Like to Thank the Academy.* Their trajectory changed.

Pay attention! Mace wanted to shout. *We're going to veer into the ocean!*

But the vehicle course-corrected on its own, without Hightower's hands touching the wheel. Thad barely glanced away from his movie.

Mace's eyes exploded to the size of dollar coins. Autopilot! Trimorphers *weren't allowed* to have autopilot features.

If President Gimbal knew about this, she'd have Hightower banned from ever racing again.

Every year, the sport of TURBO had to battle false claims that 'nauts were little more than passengers in their vehicles. Self-driving automation represented a huge threat to the sport, in the same way that steroids threatened the integrity of cycling or professional baseball. No one cares about races involving robot vehicles. Who wants to watch a basketball game where a robot point guard makes full-court shots every time it gets the ball?

But Mace had always dismissed the threat. The idea of truly autonomous racers was absurd. A program could certainly land a trimorpher, or, say, fly one across the Drake Passage, but it could never outsmart the instinct of a human being, not in the context of a professional race.

Hightower's character in "Blind Allie" walked into a pole. The joke here, Mace figured, was that Hightower's character wasn't the blind one. The real Hightower howled with laughter.

Mace shrank back in his hiding space, disgusted. *He's laughing at his own dumb movie. Am I going to have to sit through the whole stupid thing?*

"You ever notice how no one uses the bathroom in movies?" Hightower's sighted character asked the titular Allie before walking into the ladies' room of a restaurant.

Hightower doubled over in his seat. "Stop it! Stop it!" he told the film.

A while later Mace could feel the craft slow. They were descending.

Refueling?

He stole a glance out the canopy and wasn't sure he trusted what his eyes were telling him. Nothing but ocean out there. An angry, heaving ocean. The waves rolled and pulsed up and down, like pistons of some planetary engine. Fierce winds grabbed the wave crests and flung them toward the sky, creating a torrent of white foam and salty spray that buffeted *Academy*'s exterior. Large seabirds seemed at home on the open expanse of rising and falling water. They'd somehow learned to fly inches from the changing ocean surface without ever touching it or flapping their wings. A hundred miles or more out to sea, and they seemed right at home.

Academy continued to drop. A wall of water stories high rushed at them, and with perfect timing—and no assistance from Thad—the trimorpher morphed into a sub, punching through the moving wall. Without smart cushioning to absorb the blow, Mace was thrown back and forth. His recently broken arm screamed out in newfound pain, and Caballero's helmet banged against a steel casing, rattling his head. A cacophony of groaning and creaking coming from all directions masked the sharp knock.

Mace was seized by an overwhelming sense of helplessness. He blinked away tears. He felt dizzy . . . out of control. As he braced himself with both forearms, favoring one over the other, he let out an involuntary yell.

Oblivious, Hightower rocked back and forth in his seat, laughing hysterically. He had no idea that Mace was with him.

Mace couldn't believe it. He drew in a deep, astounded breath. But then he understood: Thad's helmet was feeding him the audio from his film, and his laughter had drowned Mace out.

Mace couldn't help but laugh.

They descended another thirty feet below the surface and leveled off. Mace gathered his calm. The sloshing and churning of the waves could still be felt down here, but the forces were no longer violent or out of sync. They were powerful and carried a rhythm Mace could anticipate. He focused on the ebb and flow—the breathing—of the ocean, and as he did so, he grew more at ease.

The water was a dark blue-gray, receiving no assistance from a low-angle sun masked by slate-bellied clouds. But it was crystal clear, and it seemed infinite in all directions.

The vehicle shot forward, and Mace watched the docking apparatus appear out of the dark blue. A thick cable tethered the station in place. It descended into the depths below.

Academy slowed. With scarcely a tap, giant pincers clamped down on the hull.

Incredible.

The movie cut off, replaced by a graphic of their docking

sequence. Thaddeus tapped his display screens, totally unengaged in the fantastic events unfolding around them. "Movie, please! Movie? Come on!"

The automatic fueling began. Mace used his phone to snap several pictures of the fueling station, which made him think of a huge skeleton, as if he were looking at it from inside the rib cage.

Hightower grumbled. He tapped several icons on his displays, swiped through a few screens, and settled on a monitor displaying a Sudoku. Mace stared in quiet fascination as Thad proceeded to fill in the puzzle's missing numbers incorrectly.

The fueling completed. The pincer arms of the station released, and *I'd Like to Thank the Academy* immediately began to sway with the surge. The sub propelled forward, accelerating as it rose.

In another minute they were airborne, soaring into the gray sky, eventually piercing the cloudy ceiling to continue south. The wintery South Pole sun hovered low on the horizon, seeming eager to set even though it was only midday.

Mace felt a familiar thrill flow through his core. *Speed.*

////// CHAPTER SIXTEEN

Academy's air-to-ground morph startled Mace out of his doze. He glanced over the seat back to determine who was behind the landing: Hightower or the autopilot. The answer was clearly the latter. Thad was too busy bumbling his way through another onscreen Sudoku puzzle to be bothered with something as technical as a rugged Antarctic landing.

The inside surfaces of the canopy were fogged over, but it seemed to Mace that it was also foggy outside. Huge snowflakes mutely hammered the glass. The fuel gauge was empty again, which suggested the underwater fueling port was the halfway point along their flight. *This ain't Florida,* he figured. *Are we really in Antarctica?* He felt a pang of pride shoulder its way up through the underlying worry that'd been gnawing at him. *That's all seven continents. Next stop: the moon.*

"You have to get out of here alive first," he mouthed into the helmet.

But again, where was here?

He could feel the tires roll over some kind of asphalt, but the roadster was slowing quickly. That probably meant they were on a runway.

He was right. *Academy* made a sharp turn and drove itself toward a hangar bay door that suddenly materialized through the snow flurry. They were inside the bay and pulling to a full stop before Mace could make heads or tails of his surroundings.

At the moment he was fixated on the handling of the autopilot. Mace had been a passenger in a number of self-driving cars recently. Every automatic car he'd been in had been programmed to operate cautiously. They were no fun. *Academy* was different. She'd even taxied off the runway and over to the hangar a little too fast.

Mace wondered: had *Academy* been on autopilot when

they first took off, too? Not wanting to move a muscle lest he be discovered, he hadn't paid attention then. The handling hadn't felt odd because he'd simply assumed Hightower was at the helm.

Mace was so troubled by the idea that the roadster itself had fooled him back in Punta Arenas that he was convinced there must be another explanation. It just wasn't possible for the autopilot to *have fun* on the road.

Or . . . was it?

Infinite Dynamic . . . Tomorrow's intelligence. Applied today.

Hightower groaned, startling Mace out of his thoughts. The canopy opened with a hiss, and the actor raised his arms, stretching. With the dark glass lifted, the interior of a large warehouse was revealed. The air was frigid.

A man in an orange coverall entered the hangar through a door, and Mace ducked, losing his view.

The seating released Hightower, and he sprang out of the cockpit, continuing to stretch ostentatiously while grunting. "Hate being stuffed in there for so long," he told the approaching person. "You wouldn't believe how bad I have to pee!"

Tell me about it, Mace thought.

"What're you whining for? The trip wasn't much longer than a qualifier."

"Races are interesting," Hightower answered. "I have things to look at." He cracked himself up, laughing. "Can you close the bay door already?" He suddenly snapped. "It's an icebox in here."

Mace heard the other man slap a button somewhere. Then the sound of automatic barn doors sliding shut drowned out all other noises for the next ten seconds.

Mace hugged his knees and rubbed his upper arms. It was as cold as a freezer in here.

"He's waiting for you," the other man said. "Go on in. We'll get this fueled up and get to work on the actuator."

"Wait, he's not sending me back *tonight*, is he?" asked Hightower coolly.

The mechanic didn't sound like he was interested in the subject one way or the other. "I dunno. He just told me to be fast."

"No," Hightower announced firmly. "I'm not getting back in that thing so quick."

"Talk to him about it," the other guy told Thad. "I'm just doing my job."

"I need a proper meal. You should see what the locals eat in Punta Arenas. I'm sick of having real food flown to me from LA."

"Uh, okay. You know I'm Chilean, right?"

Mace heard Hightower's familiar boots stride off across the floor. "Good for you! Upload more me-movies onto the hard drive, okay? For the ride back. Be sure to include my Christmas special." Mace heard a door click shut.

"Stupid rich blowhard," the mechanic muttered as he wheeled a spherical mobile fuel tank toward the craft.

He was still cursing Hightower as he opened the jet fuel port and coupled a nozzle to it.

Mace listened as the vehicle filled with fuel, paralyzed with indecision and mounting worry.

He had to get out of here. But how? And when?

If Hightower was spending the night somewhere before departing, Mace could literally freeze to death waiting for him to come back. He knew his best bet was to wait here in the hopes that Hightower would return to Chile as soon as the actuator was replaced. But then Mace would have come all the way to Antarctica and learned squat about whatever was going on with *I'd Like to Thank the Academy*. If he did nothing else, he needed to get pictures of the hangar bay he was in.

A door opened and closed. Other than the sound of pumping fuel, all was suddenly quiet. Mace risked popping his head up for a better look around.

The mechanic had left, and the hangar was still.

Mace sprang from the cockpit. There was no telling how long the mechanic or others would be gone. He locked the only door in, and then dragged a heavy workbench in front of it.

While he waited for the fueling to stop, he took dozens of photos of the large hangar bay with his phone. He captured everything on the benches lining the walls, taking particular interest in some of the computer workstations labeled with Infinite Dynamic logos. A fleet of snowcats, snowmobiles, and tender boats were parked in the darkness of a connected receiving bay. He snapped a few shots of those then took a couple panoramas of the whole garage. The name Infinite Dynamic was on almost everything. He'd sort the details out later.

But more important, he needed a bathroom.

Seeing no other options, he found a snowcat parked in

the back and took care of business behind it.

The fueling apparatus clicked off.

Mace pocketed the phone safely in an inside flap of his flight gear. He darted over to the mobile fuel tank and decoupled the nozzle, letting the hose drop to the floor. He lifted himself up and studied cockpit dashes for a long, steady beat.

The roadster was ready to drive. Everything else looked in order, too.

"Am I doing this?" *It'll be* you *behind the wheel.* . . .

A wave of fear filled him with mild nausea.

"Do I have a choice?"

He thought he could do it.

He realized his nerves weren't simply about a lack of confidence in himself. He'd have to refuel in the ocean or he'd die. The autopilot knew the coordinates, but what if he missed finding the submersed fueling dock by even half a degree?

Someone tried to open the door, found it locked, and gave it a hard rattle.

"Go time!" Mace told himself. If Hightower could watch a movie while automated systems did all the work, then Mace should be able to figure out what to do.

He ran over to the barn-door button and punched it.

A blast of icy air rushed in through the widening gap. Near white-out conditions swirled violently outside, and snow billowed into the hangar bay.

Mace had no time to second-guess his decision. He bolted for the trimorpher, leaped inside, took the seat, and pressed the canopy closed. The ignition obeyed his touch.

He was terrified, but his hesitancy to launch into a gathering blizzard was trumped by the simple need to escape.

The door blocked by the workbench pushed open in three successive forceful blows. The orange-coveralled mechanic took one look at Mace's helmet just as the tinted canopy lowered shut. "Caballero? You broke out *again*?"

Mace gasped. *Dex is here?*

Four other figures dressed in orange piled into the garage, all agape. Thaddeus Hightower appeared at the threshold only to be shoved aside by a much larger man, broad-shouldered, with a graying crew cut and firmly pressed white camo military fatigues.

That man reached over and slammed his open palm against the barn-door button. "Get him! Now!" he shouted.

Mace recognized his voice: this was the man who had instructed Hightower to come here.

Mace hit the gas while cranking the emergency brake and turning sharply. The donut circles were tight and precise. Squealing tires generated thick black smoke, which mixed with the incoming gusts of snow. His would-be attackers backed away, shying their faces. Mace timed the end of his hot-rodding so that *Academy*'s nose was facing the closing bay doors, and he gunned it for the white world beyond.

The gap between barn doors was shrinking quickly! But Mace had developed a trademark namesake maneuver for just such occasions. With the deft push of a few buttons, he executed a flawless "Renegade Roll"—extending only one wing so that *Academy* tilted high off its two left wheels—and shot to freedom at full speed.

The extended wing retracted, and *Academy* fell back on all four wheels. But now what? He couldn't see anything. The ground was a white plain with dancing eddies of snowdrifts, set against a backdrop of dense fog and blowing snow. He slowed down, unsure even where the asphalt beneath him might end. Running himself into a ditch would get him nowhere fast. He crept forward, watching the pavement stretch out before him as best he could.

Smoke rose from the seams around *Academy*'s hood. The actuator was calling it quits. *I gotta get out of roadster form.*

Two motorcycles with heavily bundled riders came up beside him, tracking him. One of them darted in front of him and slowed. They were trying to herd him. He veered out of the way and gave *Academy* a little bit of gas.

"Let's see what this autopilot can do." He navigated the displays while blindly barreling forward, hoping for something obvious to pop out at him. "Return to Punta Arenas," he said out loud. That didn't help. But then he saw a Destinations icon and tapped it. There it was: "Drake Passage Fueling Port."

Mace stabbed it.

The screens changed, and he could feel the roadster taking control. There was an additional burst of speed, a correction to the left . . . Mace released his hands from the wheel, looked out at the blinding snow, and laughed with nervous delight.

The roadster was driving itself—fast—and it seemed to know where it was going through the zero-visibility whiteout.

He was definitely on a runway. The roadster was gathering speed, driving arrow straight. Black smoke mixed with his view of the blizzard. Any second now, he'd sprout wings and would truly be free. He'd call the police from the air, turn the vehicle in to the Association for inspection, hand over Dex's helmet as evidence.

Thaddeus Hightower's unlikely reign over the sport would be history. All the actor's wins would be erased from the books!

Most importantly, he'd get help so Dex could be rescued.

He watched out his windows as the motorcycles flanking him arced wide, veering off the runway. As they did so, they . . . morphed into snowmobiles!

"That's pretty cool" Mace conceded.

All of a sudden, *I'd Like to Thank the Academy* braked hard and whipped around. She resumed driving immediately, but in the exact wrong direction.

"Wait. What are you doing?" Mace shouted. In a panic, he tried swiping through screens and navigating command prompts, but the monitors flashed off, denying him input. "Hey, knock it off. Come back on!" The vehicle ignored his shouted orders.

Mace gripped the wheel and pressed down on the brake pedal. But the roadster pushed back. It wouldn't respond to his tugging, turning, or kicking. The controls were beyond his physical strength to alter. His tender side was starting to hurt from the effort.

What kind of autopilot is this?

I'd Like to Thank the Academy re-entered the hangar while Mace begged and pleaded with it to relinquish control. Instead, the smart cushioning redoubled its grip on his legs, arms, and torso. The roadster halted. The canopy glass lifted. Mace was trapped. Only his hands were free to move. He felt like he was locked in carbonite. There was nothing he could do.

The snowmobiles returned to the bay, transforming back into motorcycles when the drivers passed over the concrete floor. A dozen or so people standing in a large semicircle glowered at him. The tall man in the snow camo fatigues marched forward. Thad Hightower stayed back.

The man loomed over him. Mace couldn't budge; the seating wouldn't release him. "I'll take this, thank you." The man removed Mace's helmet—Dex's helmet—and studied the newly revealed boy for several long seconds.

"Mace Blazer," the figure said. "What in the hell am I supposed to do with you?"

"Let me go!" Mace demanded, struggling to free an arm or a leg, but he was no match against the pressure of the hardened foam encasing him.

"I can't do that, Renegade," the man confessed. He almost seemed as if he genuinely regretted his answer. "You've seen too much. Far too much."

"What have you done with Dex?"

The man reached into the cockpit and held his finger on one of the light displays. "Time for you to take a nap," he said.

Mace felt the smart cushioning grow tighter, like a doctor pumping too much air into a blood pressure cuff. "Stop it," he struggled to say. The seating was pressing in on his lungs, crushing his already tender ribs. He called out in pain and couldn't draw in a new breath.

"Nighty-night," the man replied, watching Mace closely.

Mace had no air. The seat squeezed and squeezed, sending the blood in his veins to the only place it could go: his head. He felt suddenly warm, then dizzy. He was fading.

And then he blacked out.

CHAPTER SEVENTEEN //////

Mace came to sometime . . . later. He was alone in a small, square room. No windows. No cameras. One exposed fluorescent light flickered above, which didn't help his pounding headache any.

He rose to his feet. The ache in his recently broken ribs was much worse, but he struggled through the pain. He was unsteady at first but found his footing. He felt along the walls and knocked gently on the wooden door. When no one answered, he gave the door a hard shake. The doorframe and knob were reinforced. He'd have an easier time of punching through the drywall than kicking down the door. *Still*, Mace thought with a tinge of hopefulness, *I could pull this drywall apart if I have to. This isn't a prison cell.*

But then what? Jog through the snow to the ocean and take a long swim?

He sat down, tenderly nursing his ribs. He noticed the chill in the room for the first time.

I'm somewhere in Antarctica, but I have no idea where.

Antarctica was significantly larger than Australia. It'd be like pinning his location down to being somewhere in the United States or Canada.

Instinctively, he reached for his phone so he could pinpoint his location on the map. It was gone. He patted his chest pockets, then unzipped them and fished around. He checked all his pockets. Nothing. They'd confiscated it.

All the photos he'd taken: what was the use?

He shouldn't have spent all that time in the hangar snapping pics during *Academy*'s fueling. They probably had cell coverage there. He could've texted his parents or called the authorities. But now it was too late.

What would he have told them, though? He *still* had no clue what was going on.

He drilled in on his thoughts. *Let's start with what you do know. Think.*

This place was run by a company called Infinite Dynamic. They made satellites and nanotech.

"What's it got to do with Hightower, though?" *I'd Like to Thank the Academy* had illegal autopilot software installed. Was Rad Thad simply a customer? Paying top dollar to fulfill a TURBO racing dream he could never achieve on his own?

Hightower. Mace's thinking lingered on the actor. The truth about him was starting to congeal: Hightower had never been a TURBOnaut. *All he does is sit in that seat and watch movies.* He wasn't simply cheating. He wasn't even racing! *He's a total fraud.*

But why would he go through all the effort of pretending to be the best TURBOnaut in the world? It was possible that Hightower was delusional enough to do that just for the sake of doing it, but Mace could sense a more logical explanation dancing just out of reach. It had something to do with the snow-camo guy. Mr. Infinite Dynamic Snow Fort General was clearly the dude in charge here. Hightower was no premium customer—he'd been taking orders, not giving them.

Mace combed his fingers though his hair, thinking hard.

And then he finally made the connection.

He's an actor. He was hired to play a part.

Mace leaned back against the wall, soaking up the truth of it.

But if Hightower was just playing a role, what was the story?

A chill that had nothing to do with his polar location swept through him. "The story is *Academy*," Mace stated.

I'd Like to Thank the Academy could drive on its own. It won most of the races it was in . . . with Hightower just sitting in there. That meant one of two things, both impossible in Mace's judgment: either Infinite Dynamic was perfecting drone racing with an expert remote pilot—maybe the snow-camo dude himself?—or it was advancing the ball on AI—artificial intelligence—decades ahead of anyone else.

The doorknob rattled. Mace heard a key slide into a lock. The military man opened the door and stood looming over him. "I'm sorry for the way I treated you," he offered in a genuinely conciliatory tone. "It was for your own safety. I needed you out of the cockpit, and it was just the easiest solution."

"Who are you?" Mace demanded.

"I'm Evander Sentinel the third. I'm a retired submarine

commander. I'm not a bad guy, Mace."

"Then let me go."

"I'll let you out. If you promise to chill a bit."

"Fine," Mace said. "But let me *leave*; otherwise this is kidnapping."

Sentinel leaned against the doorframe. "Are you out of your mind, son? No one brought you here against your will. You're a stowaway. *You're* in a lot of trouble. You don't have clearance to be here. You shouldn't even know this place exists. I'm just trying to figure out what to do now that you do."

Mace shook his head. "You knocked me out."

"You could've run over my men with your crazy stunts!" Sentinel yelled. "I neutralized a threat!" He backed off, seeming upset with himself for his outburst. He tried again. "Now, can I let you out of here? Are you going to be reasonable?"

"Are you going to give me some answers?"

Sentinel let his amusement show. "Answers? Like to what?"

"Are you holding Caballero here? And Katana, too?"

"I don't know what you're talking about."

"I want to see my friends."

"Do I look like a day-camp counselor to you?"

The commander's attitude made Mace angry. "Here's a question. Is *Academy* controlled by remote, or by AI? And why are you trying to win the Prix with it?"

Sentinel frowned. "Why would I let you go, when you'd run off spouting theories like those?"

Mace winced. "Um, because you'll get another fancy merit badge for your chest rack there?" he tried.

"Get used to the cold," Sentinel concluded.

"I won't go to the authorities," Mace bargained.

"The authorities." Sentinel laughed. "Who do you think I work for, kid? The government paid for this installation. It's top secret. The only 'authorities' who could help you are the same folks who'll never admit this place exists."

As Mace thought about that, it started to sink in that no one would ever find him. He was going to have to escape this place on his own.

Sentinel closed the door hard. Mace heard him slip a key into the knob and lock it, and then he walked away, leaving Mace with nothing but silence.

Mace had always thought he hated silence. He was about to find out just how much.

CHAPTER EIGHTEEN /////

The door opened. Mace awoke and shot to his feet.

"I like what you've done with the place," Sentinel said.

Mace had been locked up throughout the night and had literally torn his room apart looking for a way out. Finding cinder blocks behind the drywall for his efforts had come as a tough blow.

"What time is it?" Mace asked.

"Oh nine hundred hours," Sentinel answered. "Storm's passed. Sun's finally rising. I thought you'd like a tour."

Sentinel smiled brightly and stepped out of the way, holding the door open.

Mace entered the hallway, absorbing everything he saw. The corridor had several doors spaced evenly along either side. At the end of the hall was a large, open common room, with couches and tables and bookshelves and a television. A kitchen and dining table were recessed farther back.

Hightower was eating a sandwich in the dining area. He waved at Mace with his mouth full.

"I want you out of here," Sentinel told him.

"Aye, aye, cap'n!" Hightower saluted, spitting bread as he spoke.

"Don't call me captain."

"My back is killing me, Ev! You can't stuff me in that crammed seat without at least a few more hours—"

"The press has already noticed Blazer and those other two are missing. They're going to ask about you too! Get. Going."

Hightower gulped down the last of his mouthful of food. "I always love our chats, Ev. You're such an inspiration. Remember our arrangement, okay?"

"When have I ever broken my word? Just keep your

mouth shut, okay? Prix's in two days. I don't want you draw-ing any more attention to yourself. Do you hear? Look at the headache it's causing me." He yanked on Mace's arm, demonstrating Exhibit A of his case. "And don't call me Ev."

"He's right," Mace said. "I'm here because I knew some-thing was fishy about you."

"Hi, Mace. I hope you enjoy your extended stay here at Bottom of the World Luxury Inn and Suites. I'll make sure Commander Evander provides you with my full library of films to watch while you're here."

"Don't rhyme my name like that, either," Sentinel said.

"You're no fun." Hightower pouted.

Mace's eyes narrowed. "Just know, Rad Thad, that *I* know you're a fraud. Everything you've ever said is a lie."

Hightower frowned.

"Get back to Chile," Sentinel told him, and then he roughly escorted Mace farther down the hall, through a door, and into the hangar.

I'd Like to Thank the Academy was in roadster form, facing the closed barn doors. Next to it was parked a large white-camo snowcat.

The snowcat had a cabin like a truck, though the windows

were bigger and more boxy, like those found on large tractors. But it didn't have wheels. Instead, it rode on continuous tracks, or tank treads. This allowed the vehicle to maneuver over the surface of deep snow in spite of its substantial weight.

They approached the snowcat. "Jump in," Sentinel instructed. Mace had to use handholds and ladder rungs to climb up to the door. He slipped inside and sidled along the bench seat. The commander piled in after him.

"Take us to Research and Development," Sentinel said. He winked at Mace. "Straight-line approach."

The snowcat rumbled to life and headed for the exit of its own accord.

"So, it's AI," stated Mace.

Sentinel smiled. "Remote-controlled drones are so Y2K. Welcome to the next era."

The hangar doors opened.

"Oh. Wow," Mace said.

He'd always pictured Antarctica in his head as a desolate wasteland: windswept, devoid of life, flat and featureless. His arrival late the previous afternoon during white-out conditions seemed to confirm those ideas: Antarctica was a barren slab of rock covered by dull white ice and snow, where the wind could knock you off your feet and freeze your eyeballs to glass marbles.

But that wasn't the world laid out before him this morning.

The weather was clear and calm. The sun was low in the sky but bright, bringing color and texture to everything on the landscape. The snow was a soft, inviting white, but that was only at the surface. There was a hint of neon blue lying just below the snow's exterior. Cracks and fissures along the snowy crust glowed a deep azure from within.

They were on a hilly island surrounded by glassy, dark blue ocean, as smooth and calm as a mirror surface. Puffy, dark-bellied clouds hovered low in the sky. The clouds were constantly changing shape as they drifted past.

The water was peppered with icebergs, beautiful sculptures in every shape imaginable, carved with deep blue pockets. The still water revealed how the icebergs were much bulkier below the surface than above, reaching down into the ocean's inviting crystal-blue depths. And the icebergs' underbellies shone an otherworldly aquamarine color Mace had never seen.

The island was large, with a crescent bay, marked by steep, snowcapped bluffs and rocky black cliffs. Surrounding them were other mountainous islands.

"You like it?" Sentinel asked proudly, as if he'd designed the scenery himself.

Mace openly admitted his astonishment. "I've never seen anything like this."

Automated snowplows and deicers cleared the runway. The short road ahead of them was already uncovered. Mace was only a little surprised when the snowcat continued straight beyond the end of the road, climbing the snow and ice as it set off across the rolling white hills toward their unseen destination.

"Does your whole fleet use AI?" Mace asked, glancing back for one last look at the unmanned machines shoveling the landing strip and taxiway.

"That's the goal," Sentinel said.

A moment passed in silence as they trod over the snow in a straight line. Mace looked beyond the scenery and studied the island's layout. They were at one end of the crescent-moon shore. The snowcat was pointed straight toward the far horn of the moon shape, which was marked by a sheer black granite cliff rising out of the blue, maybe five hundred feet high over the water. Mace guessed other facilities must lie on the far side of that towering formation.

All along the length of the snow-covered beaches, the ground was riddled with black dots. Much of the snow was discolored a rusty pink for some reason.

"Is that all you're going to tell me?" he pressed.

"You want answers, then I need to know you can stay silent."

Mace shook his head. "I don't like silence."

Sentinel studied him, and Mace thought he saw respect in the man's eyes. "I knew you'd be lying if you'd said anything different. But there's time. You may come around. I might just impress you."

Mace wasn't going to beg for answers. He was looking forward, wondering when the snowcat would start to veer and follow the curvature of the island. Their current trajectory would have them in the water in a few seconds. Maybe the AI was malfunctioning.

"I am impressed," Mace said. "For a long time I didn't realize Hightower wasn't in control of *I'd Like to Thank the Academy.*"

"That's the standard we're reaching for," Sentinel replied. "But you haven't seen anything yet."

The snowcat kept plowing straight toward the water. Mace braced for impact, wondering how cold the water would feel as they blindly tumbled into the ocean. The surface was so still he could see how the AI might not register land's end. . . .

But the morph was perfectly timed. Suddenly, Mace was a passenger on a tender boat skimming over the water before he fully understood what had happened. The straight-line trajectory proceeded across the ocean's surface unhindered. "It's a morpher!" he cried. "Amphibious."

Commander Sentinel smiled quietly, sitting back in his seat.

Mace was startled by a great deal of splashing along the water's surface. He looked closely as the ruckus drew nearer. *Fish?* he thought at first. *A school of flying fish?* It was a group of small animals of some kind. But the swimmers were too fat to be fish. They were too small to be dolphins. And then he figured it out.

"Penguins!"

Mace watched them go by, bloated and happy on their

way to shore after feeding on fish farther out in the deep bay. He realized the black dots he'd noticed earlier—the thousands of them peppered all along the uneven shore—were penguins too. The island was swarming in penguins. And the pink, rusty color beneath them—penguin poop.

"All right, Mace," warned Sentinel. "We're getting close to your new home. Lean all the way back in your seat; put the straps on."

Mace took the advice. The tender boat had motored right up to the cliff face, still traveling perfectly straight. *Is it a dicer too?* He figured they were going to lift straight up out of the water on helicopter blades now. But he was wrong.

Instead, the transforming vehicle sprouted spidery legs and began to walk up the cliffside. Mace was suddenly flat on his back, looking at the sky as the transport crawled up the wall.

Sentinel laughed and pressed a button. The seats quickly adjusted to the new gravity vector, swiveling upright, with the glass roof of the cabin now a vertical window offering a dizzying view of the crescent island and the bay and other tall islands in the distance.

Mace looked out at the landscape, feeling like he was

ascending a skyscraper in a glass elevator.

"With such rough weather coming and going without a moment's notice around here, we've found legs to be much more useful and safe than wings for getting over obstacles. Imagine if the Allied forces had a fleet of these on D-Day."

But Mace was hardly listening to the commander. He was kind of freaking out, sure that their pod was about to lose its grip and plummet into the bay. They summited the rocky spire and descended the far side. The seats swiveled and turned, orienting to the new down. The far side of the ridge wasn't as steep, and Mace relaxed his muscles, but just a little. He could see a structure down by the coast, or maybe several. Everything was painted white, and all he could make out was vague geometric shapes that didn't quite fit with the rest of the landscape.

Finally, the spider legs touched down on solid, flat ground. The vehicle leaned forward before morphing back into a snowcat.

The vehicle slowed as it approached the compound, pulling into a new hangar as if completing a lazy Sunday drive. Sentinel parked in an empty bay slot among other snowcats, and the garage door shut.

"What do you think? Any change of heart?" Sentinel asked as they climbed down from the snowcat.

"I'm not your friend. I'm not your puppet. And I'll never work for you," Mace said.

"I'm offering you a chance, Mace. Partnership is your only exit plan," Sentinel said, escorting Mace inside the building. This compound was different from the runway facility. Mace could sense, just from the echoes in the hall, that it was much more extensive, with multiple stories. He could hear voices, chairs squeaking, doors opening and closing. It was an active place, with lots of people striding to and fro. He heard computers humming, keyboards typing, and server banks etching data. He thought he could hear an arc welder somewhere around an echoing corner.

While the first building was merely a quiet airport terminal and way station with a kitchen and simple lodgings, this place was filled with purpose.

"I'm playing host to some other long-term visitors, as you've already guessed," Sentinel continued, ushering Mace quickly into a utility elevator occupied by a guy shuttling a cart stacked with industrial equipment. They descended one floor to the basement level, and Sentinel led Mace through another long hall. He used a keycard to open a secure, metal door. "It's getting a bit crowded. It's a shame. So much talent to offer, yet you're all too idealistic to see what you're missing out on."

The commander gave Mace a shove through the doorway. "Enjoy your accommodations." And without even a goodbye, Sentinel slammed the door shut.

Mace heard a deadbolt slide into place. The lock clicked with a beep. Mace noted quickly that it wasn't the kind of lock he'd be able to hack.

"I ask for someone to play cards with," a familiar male voice grumbled, "and this is who they send?"

Mace slowly turned around.

Seated at a table just past a kitchenette area, rows deep into a card game of solitaire, was Dex.

CHAPTER NINETEEN //////

"There you are!" Mace complained. "You're a hard man to find."

Dex stood to greet him. His metal dining chair scraped on the concrete floor. Mace noticed that his friend's leg was handcuffed to it. The padlock required a key. "What's this?"

"My new cochair." Dex sighed.

"Okay. Makes sense. Where's Aya?"

"She's here," Dex confirmed. "But not *here*. We launched an escape just about the second she got here. After that, Sentinel chained me to this chair, and they whisked Aya to some other room. This place was never intended to be a prison, so they're figuring it out as they go."

"We may not have long, then," Mace said, "before they separate us too. So, how do we get out of here?"

"Mace, look." Dex pointed to his cuffed ankle. The chair was heavy but unrestrained. He could move freely around the quarters, but he wouldn't get far through the rest of the facility—at least not quietly—dragging a chair behind him.

"We'll figure it out," Mace assured his friend.

"I've tried it all," Dex replied unhelpfully. "But the problem is that once you get outside, then what? There's no escape; we're stuck until they decide to let us go." He sat down next to the kitchenette counter.

"No," Mace said. "We need to hack into the system. Steal a vehicle."

"You don't think I tried that?"

Mace didn't care. He put his ear to the door, then to the keypad by the knob, feeling along every surface within his reach. The walls were covered with a stucco finish, but were clearly made of cinder blocks beneath. The electrical outlets and switches were all externally mounted on the wall, with the wiring housed in protective steel tubes, further proof that the walls were solid everywhere. No chewing through this material. The wiring for the ceiling lights and fans was also external, dashing Mace's hopes of a false ceiling with a crawl space above them. He moved on to study the rest of the room. The area felt like a loft apartment. The living room was sizable, and there was an open-layout kitchen with a fridge and a gas stove and a couple of pantry cabinets. Mace noticed a bedroom beyond.

No windows anywhere, though, and no other doors except to the bathroom. Mace didn't give up. He scanned the bookshelves, felt along the walls, flipped the light switches, checked behind the toilet.

"What're you doing, Mace? I've been locked in here for days. We're underground. You don't think I've tried every-thing?"

"Maybe you missed something," he told Dex, pulling books off the shelf to investigate the wall.

"And you're going to waltz in here and 'voilà!'" He snapped his fingers. "'Oh, look here, Dex, you missed this secret tunnel leading to California over here behind the dic-tionary.'"

"How'd you end up here?" Mace asked, continuing to

scan and to feel around the room.

"I found out Thad Hightower was just a passenger in his trimorpher. Caught him getting into *Academy after* it pulled out of the warehouse. I couldn't believe it, but he saw me watching. The next thing I remember . . . I was here."

Dex stumbled through his thoughts. He rubbed the back of his head. "Someone hit me on the head. I don't know who. But when Aya got here, she told me she followed *my* crew chief here. He was delivering *Silverado*. Erasing evidence."

Mace stopped looking behind books. "Wait. Why?"

"To make it look like I had taken off on my own, I'm guessing," Dex explained. "No one will believe I was kidnapped if they can make the claim I ran off because of nerves or I died at sea in my own morpher."

Mace nodded hesitantly. "But, so . . . your crew chief is working for them?"

"Sounds like it." Dex heaved a sigh. "But don't look at me. Olesya hired my crew. She said he came highly recommended."

"Wow," Mace said. "Sentinel really has this planned out."

Dex left the kitchen area and walked himself and his chair closer to Mace. He sat back down. "How much do you know? About Hightower? About what Sentinel is doing?"

Mace stopped his search for tunnels to California. He sat down on the couch opposite Dex and took a deep breath. "I know *I'd Like to Thank the Academy* is run by some kind of artificial intelligence."

"Yeah, but why is Sentinel running AI in the TURBO league to begin with?"

"That I don't know," admitted Mace. "He said he'd only tell me if I agreed to partner with him."

Dex barked laughter. "That's what he told me. So I said I would. Then he explained what he's up to. And then I went, 'No way I'm helping you with that!' And now I have this chair."

"So what did he say he was doing?"

Dex took a deep breath. "Have you heard of Alan Turing?" he asked.

"No."

"He was an early computer science pioneer. Back in the 1940s and '50s, back before our modern idea of computers was around. But he predicted a lot about computers. And robots. He was a code-breaker during World War II, and he invented equations and algorithms to help early computers break enemy codes. Anyway, he thought a lot about artificial intelligence, and he invented the Turing test."

"What is it?" asked Mace.

"It involves the idea that a machine can be said to have 'intelligence' if it can fool humans into thinking it's also human. So, for example, imagine you're texting or emailing back and forth with two people. But one of the people is a human and the other is a computer program pretending to be human. If you can tell which is which, then the program isn't advanced enough to fool you. But if you can't tell them apart . . ."

"Then the machine passes the Turing test," Mace finished for him.

"You've got it," Dex said.

"So, Sentinel is developing machines that can beat human 'nauts in a Gauntlet Prix without anyone catching on. But why does he need to fool audiences into thinking Hightower's the pilot?"

Dex had an answer. "Because the Association would never allow an automated racer in the league. Using Hightower as a front is the only way to get *Academy* in the lineup."

"Makes sense," Mace told him. "But the question is why do this *at all*? You think Sentinel's after a sports trophy because his awards display case has an empty shelf?"

Dex rubbed his cuffed ankle. "He's a retired navy sub-marine commander. He's working on a government contract with the military, operating out of a top secret base. The endgame can only be one thing, right?"

Mace shot up. "Oh, man," he said. Out of the jumble of new information swirling in his head, he reached for the three most relevant details. "AI. Military. Trimorphers."

"Imagine the battlefield implications," Dex suggested. "Tanks that are also jets that are also submarines that can outsmart enemy fighters; the enemy unable to tell a manned craft from an unmanned craft, wasting ammo on automated targets while the troops waltz behind enemy lines . . ."

"And claim victory without taking a single bullet," Mace continued for him.

Dex nodded. "Yeah, but he's not developing toy decoys. We're talking autonomous morphing vehicles. He's manu-facturing disposable super soldiers."

"But where does TURBO racing come into this? That's what I still don't get."

"He wants to pass the Turing test, Mace. To prove the tech is ready to sell. And if you're trying to jack up your price and impress potential buyers, what bigger stage is there? No single race in the world is more complicated than a Prix."

"Wait, though: he's contracted with the US military. He can't sell it."

Dex shook his head. "That's what the government thinks. But I've seen people touring this place. I think he wants to sell his AI to the highest bidder."

"This isn't just about us," Mace concluded. The world was on the brink of a dangerous new type of arms race, and no one but Mace and Dex knew it. "We've gotta get out of here. We've gotta find Aya. Then we get this info to Gimbal and the rest of the world before the Prix."

"Hate to break it to you, dude, but the Prix's in, like, forty hours."

"Then let's get cracking."

CHAPTER TWENTY //////

Mace and Dex continued exploring and re-exploring every square inch of the operation manager's quarters, to no avail. Those who had built this place might not have had prison cells in mind, but this basement unit served as a great substitute.

No one visited them. Mace found his frustration and despair growing. How was he supposed to study the patterns of their captors for escape ideas if there was no pattern to observe? The apartment's kitchenette was stocked with a ton of food. Was it possible they'd be forgotten for days, even weeks?

Mace intensified his pacing.

Dex was at the stove, boiling water for pasta. "Get over here and slice these tomatoes. I'm not your mother. You're not getting any of this food unless you help make it."

"With what knife?" Mace asked.

"No knives here," Dex said. "But they were kind enough to leave us this wonderful wire egg-dicer-thingy. Have at it."

"Maybe we could start a fire," Mace said, watching the gas flames hiss beneath the pot. "They'd have to free us. In the confusion of putting it out, we could hijack a snowcat morpher, dart to another island and hide out until—"

"Hate to splash icy water on that," Dex said, "but I'm attached to a metal chair. I'm not darting anywhere. Let's keep fire out of it."

Icy water . . . that gave Mace another idea. "Well, let's leave the water running," he tried. "Flood the place out. When they come to see what's wrong, *I* make a break for it, then come back for you—"

"Stop it, Mace," Dex insisted. "This place has one door and it swings inward. We'd drown before they realized we needed saving. You're missing the point. Sentinel locked us up here until he can figure out what to do with us. Starting a fire or a flood will only solve his problems for him."

Mace watched the stove. The water in the pot started to boil. He stared at the rising steam, followed it up to the overhead cabinets where it entered the . . . hood.

"Hey," Mace said, rushing over and craning his neck to look up into it without touching the hot stove. "Where does that vent lead?"

Dex stood on top of his chair and opened the cabinets above the oven, revealing the wide, sheet metal chimney wall of the hood. "It goes up through the ceiling here," he explained. "But I took out the grating over the stove the first day I was here." He unscrewed the wingnuts even as he spoke and let the grating swivel and hang down over the boiling pot of water. "Look up in there. That chimney narrows to a pipe a couple feet up. We're not the Mario Brothers. There's no way a person can follow that path out."

"I can see that," Mace said. "But look. The chimney makes a big hole in the cinder-block ceiling. If we cut through the sheet metal above the ceiling line, we could access whatever's up there."

Dex squinted. "It's not a crazy idea," he concluded. Mace was glad Dex agreed. Sheet metal was no thicker than a soup can. It could be punctured with a flathead screwdriver and a hammer. There was a screwdriver in one of the drawers. And a hammer could be fashioned out of anything. There were some bookends made out of black rock on the bookshelves. That would do.

"Let me finish cooking my pasta before you destroy the kitchen," Dex suggested.

They ate before getting to work. Throughout the long polar night, they took turns standing up on the stove with their heads, arms, and torsos stuffed into the interior of the hood, puncturing holes into the sheet metal surface of the vent system. They were slow and meticulous, trying to be quiet. Toward morning, they finished the task, peeling back a square of sheet metal, revealing a darkened cinder-block gap between floors—a gap high enough to crawl through.

Mace helped Dex get down from the countertop, lowering the chair as Dex lowered himself. Dex was going to have to stay behind because of his elaborate ankle bracelet. "It's probably for the best," he offered, "if anyone comes knocking. Maybe I can convince them you're sleeping if they wonder where you are."

"I'll be speedy," Mace promised, his heart already pounding.

Dex winked back at him. "Spoken like a true TURBOnaut."

Mace climbed into the hood and stood tall, then shimmied upward a little bit and bent over so that he was squirming through the flap in the sheet metal and into the cinder-block crawl space between floors. He pulled his body forward using his hands and began to explore the dark.

He felt his way forward until a joist lined with pipes blocked his path. He followed the pipes to a brick wall. The pipes bent up through the top of the crawl space and disappeared, but each pipe was fitted with valves.

Why would there be valves here unless they could be accessed?

Mace felt along the brick wall and discovered an access panel. Bingo. Toying with the panel for just a few seconds, he was able to unlatch it and swing it open. A quiet hallway opened up on the far side. Mace cautiously poked his head through. No activity. It was morning now, but still dim. *Don't be fooled by the winter darkness.* People would be awake and going about their business.

Hurry.

Mace squirmed and squeezed his way through the opening.

Around the corner, someone was coming. He sprang to his feet in the hallway. A bulky, knee-high object turned into view. Mace almost bolted, but it was just a robot polishing the tiled floor.

He stepped out of the way as the thing moseyed past. He brushed himself off and hesitantly picked a direction, choosing to follow the robot because it could at least provide him some cover if other people appeared. He hugged the walls as the robot selected a path through the labyrinth of hallways.

Aya, where are you?

The first door he came to had a window. Mace stole a glance through the glass, recognizing a control room of some kind. He wanted a better look. The half-dozen or so computer monitors promised access to potential goodies, such as Aya's location and a map to help him get around. But two soldiers sat at the desk, entering data.

Mace took a final peek into the room. Two monitors displayed a live security feed. One of the videos showed the other facility. A single-engine plane was parked in the hangar, and it was surrounded by most of Sentinel's men, arranged in a grid around an arriving guest, visible only as a vague, pixelated figure. No wonder it felt so quiet here this morning.

The other camera was monitoring a plowed driveway outside and was aimed at a white snowcat fading off toward the far end of the island through a curtain of falling snow.

Mace ducked below the control-room window and proceeded down the hall, working his way a lengthy distance toward the next door. Three soldiers walked casually toward him. Mace kept tightly against the waist-high mop robot, staying out of view. The men passed without noticing him. The robot turned a corner, and Mace stayed with it.

The robot janitor paused at a door. There was a whirring. A diode on the mopper's upper display surface blinked. A corresponding blink came from the door lock, and the door clicked open. The robot entered the room, triggering motion sensors that turned on the lights. Mace shrugged and followed the robot inside.

He found himself in a windowed antechamber of a much larger factory floor. White ski helmets, snow masks, and snow goggles lined the shelves. Mace grabbed one of each and pulled them over his face, feeling suddenly much less vulnerable to detection. The robot docked itself and released a sigh, as if it were long overdue for a break and a recharge. Mace had no time to be amused. He grabbed a puffy snow-camo jacket. He hoped it would serve to make him seem larger.

He found a clipboard on the antechamber's wall. It showed a spreadsheet with last names, job titles, room numbers, and other numerical data.

"Interesting." Mace combed through the roster until he found two rooms that were simply listed as "occupied." He noted the room numbers. One was the basement number where Dex was, and one was labeled 138. "Worth a shot," he mumbled, tearing the sheet of paper off the clipboard and pocketing it. He studied a fire-exit map on the wall, memorizing the route to room 138, and set off.

He exited the antechamber but didn't let the door latch.

He turned a corner and ran straight into a soldier coming around the next bend.

"Easy, pardner!" the guy intoned. "You heading out?"

Mace backed off a step, a frog in his throat. He nodded.

"Where's your gloves at? Cold out there this morning."

"Uh," said Mace gruffly beneath the snow mask. "Bathroom first."

The man nodded and continued on his way.

Mace hurried around the corner, shaking off a sudden rush of adrenaline. He came to the apartment door. "Now what?" he asked the walls.

If he called for Aya and she replied, that would be one thing. But if someone else were behind the door—?

He knocked, and before he could take cover, he heard a telling reply. "What is it? I can't open the door, you know."

It was her.

Mace couldn't open the door, either. The lock had both a keypad and a slot to swipe a card, but he had neither code nor card. Unless—

"Aya. It's me."

"Mace!" she exclaimed. But she wasn't excited; she was worried. "What are you doing here?"

"I'll be right back. Be ready to go."

He scurried back down the hall toward the antechamber of the factory floor and ducked inside. The robot janitor was still docked at its charging station. Mace helped himself to the touch screen display panel, navigating menus until he found a scheduling override. He prompted the robot to clean room 138 and backed out of the way as the robot dutifully aborted its recharge and took to the hallway with cheerful purpose.

Mace waited over a minute before following. Still, he caught up to the thing well before it reached Aya's quarters.

"Hurry up," he told it. "What a time waste. This better work."

It did. When the robot reached room 138, it turned to communicate with the door. The lock chimed politely and unlatched.

Mace paused the robot. He darted inside and closed the door behind him, careful not to shut it all the way, just in case.

Aya stared at him from the hallway leading to her bedroom. She cleared her throat. "Aren't you a little short for a patrol scout?"

"Huh?" Mace asked her. And then he remembered how bundled up he was. "Oh." He ripped off the goggles and mask. "It's me. I'm here to rescue you."

"You better have a plan," she stated flatly.

"I'm working on it." Mace peeked back outside and

unpaused the robot, which entered the apartment.

"What's that?" asked Aya.

"My master key for the building." Mace reprogrammed the janitor to go clean Dex's quarters all the way back across the far corridor and down to the basement level. With unquestioning obedience, the robot did an about-face and lurched into action.

"It'll take him a minute to get there," Mace noted. "Let's get you bundled up in gear, and grab a set for Dex, too."

He led Aya through the hallways, past the advancing robot, back toward the anteroom with its masks and goggles and snow jackets.

"Where is everyone?" Aya wondered.

"Oh, there're plenty people moving around. But someone just arrived at the runway. A lot of them are over there for that."

"Probably another bidder," guessed Aya.

They slipped into the anteroom connecting to the larger factory beyond. Aya donned more layers as they kept an eye on the windows to the interior of the larger warehouse. Her new outfit did a respectable job of disguising her.

Mace approached the window for his first detailed look

into the factory. Nearby along an automated assembly line, robotic arms were busy putting the final touches on a large, armored transport. Mace could see tank treads tucked into the interior belly of the vehicle, which meant it was undoubtedly a morpher of some kind. A scrawny man wearing a respirator stood with his back to Mace and Aya, inspecting the assembly.

Mace watched with a mechanic's fascination as two robotic arms attached a metal grill to the front of the transport truck, while other robot arms painted the exterior white. The masked inspector circled the vehicle, making notes on a clipboard.

Aya leaned in close. "What's the *plan*, Mace? What are we waiting for? Why's Dex not with you?"

"Dex is foot-cuffed to a chair downstairs. The robot needs time to get over there and unlock the door."

"I mean, how are we getting out of here?"

A storm of footsteps echoed up the hallway which they'd come from. The door behind them jostled. Aya and Mace shared a worried look and then darted forward into the assembly plant through the adjoining door. They didn't have to worry about making too much noise. The machinery was loud enough to cover them. They pressed back against the wall and shimmied behind one of the robotic arm mounts.

The arm lifted and swung in a wide arc to retrieve another armored panel with a large robot claw. Mace was about to be crushed at the base of the machine. He had to execute a perfectly timed dive roll through a hydraulic press to dodge the rotating machinery. Aya followed suit. The maneuver saved their skins: several people entered the antechamber and proceeded into the assembly plant. They would've stumbled over Mace and Aya if not for the moving equipment.

Mace watched from his new hiding spot. The lead figure was Evander Sentinel, decked out in starched white camo. Next to him stood a man and a young woman, stern-faced, beneath thick Baltic snow hats and slate-gray officers' uniforms.

The man was the self-identified king of Kreznia and the woman was his daughter, Princess Olesya Vasko.

///// CHAPTER TWENTY-ONE

"What're they doing?" Mace wondered aloud. "Is she here to negotiate our release?"

"Mace. She's not here to rescue us," Aya answered. She rolled her eyes at him for good measure.

"Then, what—?" The follow-up question died on his lips. "They're . . . shopping?"

The inspector shut off the machines and removed his mask. It was suddenly very quiet.

"This is Simon, our deputy fleet forces maintenance technician," Sentinel told the Vaskos. He turned to Simon.

"Meet His Royal Majesty Andrey Vasko of the newly declared Unified Baltic Federation, and Army General Princess Olesya Vasko."

Army General? Mace thought.

"Princess isn't enough of a title?" scoffed Aya.

"Lay off," snapped Mace. "I'm sure there's an explanation."

"Oh, there is," Aya snapped back. "They're shopping for a robot army! It explains why she was with Hightower yesterday morning. They're in this together!"

"No," Mace said. "That's not right. It can't be right."

"If Olesya were a *prince* and not a *princess* you wouldn't be so confused," Aya hissed.

"Why don't you give him my home address?" the king complained. "Blabbering to an assembly-line worker."

"I run a tight ship, your majesties. Minimal staff. Only a few dozen very loyal, trusted confidants. Simon was on my submarine crew, like most of my colleagues stationed here. You can trust any one of the men on this island."

Olesya considered the line inspector skeptically. She turned back to Evander. "Only a few dozen collaborators?"

"They're mostly back at the airstrip," Sentinel answered.

"I like to give visiting guests room to think when they make the trip all the way out here. Your bid is by far the most promising we've seen. I understand your tight schedule. I'd like to get your commitment to formalize a deal quickly."

"You have my word," stated the king. "It's based on a couple conditions, of course. And I do want to go for a spin first."

"Naturally," Sentinel answered. He put out his hand and the king shook it.

The princess tapped on her father's shoulder. "What about what we discussed? *Academy*'s victory tomorrow is a sham while the world's top three 'nauts are all sidelined. We need to see a proper matchup before we commit."

"The theatrics hardly matter at this point, love. We need the fleet delivered ASAP."

"But father, the Prix will—"

The king was losing patience. "Please, darling, enough with your TURBO obsession! If they're released, they'll talk. Sentinel, let's wrap this up, shall we?"

The ex-submarine commander smiled. "Right this way. Please. Choose anything from the fleet for your test ride. They all have equal fuel."

She knows we're sidelined, Mace's mind continued to reel. *She knows we're being held by Sentinel.* "We've got to tip her off," Mace told Aya. "She needs to know we're here. She'll help us."

"Are you out of your mind? Don't you dare," Aya insisted. "These two are on the cusp of triggering World War III. Just stay away from them. They're nothing but trouble, and they don't care at all about you or me."

The princess scowled. "Which of these can fly?" she asked the commander.

"Here?" Sentinel replied, annoyance plain in his voice. "None of them fly. Weather is too volatile, and runway space is difficult to maintain. *Lotus* and *Silverado* are parked in our small east bunker, but they're out of gas and not equipped with my software upgrades. *I'd Like to Thank the Academy* is the prototype for the fleet you'll be purchasing. She can easily house an array of weaponry in all morphs. We'll make arrangements for a test drive shortly after we receive your purchase order. The Prix is the main event. It will show that my tech can deliver everything you're looking for."

East bunker? Mace noted. *That's going to be our ticket home.*

Aya offered him a fist bump. Obviously she was thinking the same thing.

But this island was big. And frozen. They weren't going to be able to walk anywhere far. They'd have to get to the east bunker, wherever that was—with fuel enough to fill two empty morphers.

"I want to try this one," the Kreznian king suggested, pointing at the brand-new transport truck still mounted on the assembly line.

Sentinel chuckled. "The Yeti? Ah, well, this is our new edition. Bigger and better. Almost ready, but the paint is wet, and the AI isn't downloaded. She'll be my pride and joy; you certainly have an eye for the best of the best."

"What does this Yeti do?"

"Tank, sub, road transport. She can be fitted to deploy bridges too. She'll carry heavy cargo. Fuel, weapons, missile loads, troops, you name it. And she'll morph safely with a whole detachment or platoon in her belly. Very versatile. Finally, a support craft able to keep up with the frontline fleet of infantry morphers, able to lead the way where roads don't already go. They'll communicate well together, adapt as a pack. They'll be able to keep up with quickly-unfolding conditions during any combat scenario."

The Vaskos and Sentinel drifted out of earshot, strolling deeper into the factory toward the fleet garage as they conversed.

"Follow them." Aya nudged Mace forward along the wall where they were crouched. "I want to know everything we can."

They stuck to the shadows, careful to steer clear of Simon's line of sight.

With nearly everyone cleared out for the king's visit, this was the perfect time to spring Dex and discover a way out of here. They needed to be ready to scram once Dex was free; three escapees—disguised or not—wandering the facility trying to steal a vehicle—it could go wrong in so many ways.

He placed both hands on either side of the gas cap of a parked snowcat. He unzipped his puffy outer jacket and cupped an ear and a cheek along the metal surface, and let the chest of his exposed flight suit rest upon the body below the cap. He closed his eyes. Then he shoved with all his might, setting the vehicle to rocking ever so slightly. Deep within the snowcat's underbelly, he felt an answering slosh of liquid. He tried again. *About a quarter full*, he thought. He pivoted to the next jeep and repeated the entire process, confirming that it felt similarly empty. "None of them seem to have much gas," he relayed to Aya.

"The storm is building out there," Olesya pointed out. "Let's get going with the demonstration."

"We'll test these two," said Andrey Vasko, pointing out the smaller, hummer-like transports in front of him. "You follow behind us in that one."

"Very well," answered Sentinel, waving a hand in invitation for the Kreznians to board their chosen armored vehicles.

The hangar bay doors opened, and snow flurries blew in. The drawn-out dawn was muted by heavy, dark clouds and strong gusts of snow. Mace watched the three transports exit the bay in single file, morphing to snowcats as they crossed the threshold. The doors began to shut automatically.

Mace rapped Aya on the shoulder. "Now's our shot. Let's grab Dex."

"Can we fit three people in two trimorphers?" Aya asked.

Mace nodded. "I got here in the back of *I'd Like to Thank the Academy*. We can make space for guests. You're not going to like it, but we don't have much choice."

"How's that?"

Mace couldn't believe what he was saying. "Rip out the safety features from behind the ejector seat."

Aya's eyes widened. "That's insane."

"If you have any other options," Mace answered, "I'm all ears."

"Well, we can worry about it when we get to that point," said Aya. "How are we getting fuel to the east hangar? We can't risk getting over there and finding there's nothing on hand."

"Absolutely," Mace agreed again. "We have one shot at this. We can't rely on luck."

"Let's take those snowmobiles. Hitch a fuel hub behind one. We should go before the storm picks up even more."

"No." Mace frowned, remembering how his initial escape attempt in *I'd Like to Thank the Academy* had been hijacked by Sentinel's remote commands to the AI.

"What's the problem?" asked Aya.

"I'm worried these can be overridden by Sentinel," Mace said. "He stopped me from escaping in *Academy* that way. We shouldn't rely on them."

"Well." Aya blew out an explosive sigh. "What do you suggest? It's Antarctica out there."

"I have a plan," Mace said. "But first let's get Dex."

CHAPTER TWENTY-TWO /////

Two minutes later, Mace had slipped out of the cargo elevator, run down the hall, and stopped in his tracks. The robot mop was dead in the hallway, totally out of charge. He tried to turn it back on. All he needed was enough juice for it to talk to the door, but it was so dead the display wouldn't light up.

"Now what?"

He stared at the digital keypad of Dex's room and knocked on the door. "Dex, it's me."

He heard rapid movement within. A chair scraped along the floor. "Mace! You were gone for a long time. I was worried—"

"I've got Aya. Time to go." Mace thought of something. Risky. His heart started pounding. But he knew it was worth a shot. "You need to set off the fire alarm."

"Mace. Come on! We've been over this—"

"Just do it. Roll up some paper, light it on the stove, and hold it up to the detector."

"Start a fire. What could possibly go wrong?"

"Trust me. And use that chair when the firefighters get here!"

"What does that mean?"

Mace didn't answer. He retreated down the hall and hid against a hallway cabinet to wait. He heard the elevator around the corner engage. It went up . . . and then came back down. One of the control room soldiers barreled into view, heading for Dex's quarters at a full sprint. He carried a fire extinguisher. Mace crept forward. The soldier was visible at the end of the hall, his back to Mace, pounding on the door with the butt of the fire extinguisher. "What's going on in there?"

"The couch is on fire! Hurry!" Dex screamed.

Muttering angrily, the soldier swiped a keycard and threw open the door.

Now, Mace thought. *Fast!*

The would-be fireman had inched farther into the room, on alert. He heard something and whipped around, only to see Mace sprinting straight at him. He reached to slam shut the door, but Dex lifted his chained leg, picked up the chair, and brought the metal seat back down on top of the soldier's head. The blow was enough to stun the guy. He dropped the extinguisher and his keycard, losing his balance and falling backward. Dex stumbled to the ground, too.

Mace snatched up the extinguisher and let it rip, spraying foam all over the stunned soldier's face. Dex dragged himself and the chair out of the way and found his feet. Mace pulled Dex by the arm out of the room, the chair dragging behind him, and then slammed the door shut.

While the solider groaned mutely on the far side of the door, Mace punched random numbers into the keypad over and over again. Finally, the lock hissed a protest, the display reading, *ATTEMPT LIMIT REACHED. WAIT FIVE MINUTES AND TRY AGAIN.*

Mace picked up the keycard lying on the floor, still hauling the extinguisher with his other hand. "Well, we've got five minutes. Let's go."

"How am I going to get anywhere chained to this?" Dex asked.

"You'll have to carry it for now, but not for long. I have an idea."

They turned about-face and rode the cargo elevator to the ground floor. As they came around a corner, they smashed straight into another soldier. Mace's arm collided with the man's elbow, and Mace reeled backward in pain.

With another awkward leg lift, Dex swung his chair again, smashing the guard against the wall. The back of the guard's head struck the wall hard, and he fell limply to the floor.

Mace stared at the crumpled body for a second, and then sprayed him with extinguisher foam.

Dex sent his friend a wary look. "What's that supposed to accomplish? He's already out."

"Icing on top."

"Where are we going?" Dex leaned over and took the man's foam-covered gun from its holster, and then he climbed onto his chair seat and hid the weapon above the shade of the hallway's lighting fixture.

"We're meeting Aya in the fleet hangar," Mace said.

"How are we getting off Antarctica?" Dex demanded.

"*Silverado* and *Lotus*."

Dex frowned. "We need to go to the control room first," he said, searching the passed-out guard's pockets for something. "We need local override access for refueling at sea. Otherwise the commander can freeze us out."

"Good call," Mace agreed. "But we have to be fast. These guys have probably already radioed the commander. What are you looking for?"

"Handcuff keys."

"We won't need any. Promise."

They resumed their awkward shuffle with the chair in tow, leaving the second guard behind.

The control room was empty—but locked. Mace swiped the keycard. It worked. They rushed in and locked the door behind them. Dex pushed a plush leather seat away from the desk and sat down at the center console using his own chair. He inserted the keycard and started typing. "Look around for anything we can store data on," he told Mace. "Memory cube, card, disk, whatever you find."

Mace began searching through cabinets and found a plug-in external solid-state memory spike. It vaguely resembled a magic wand. "Four terabytes enough for you?"

"Perfect." Dex held one hand out for it and kept typing with the other.

"Do you have internet?" Mace asked. "We should email our families, at least."

"I don't have time," Dex said, typing. "This is more important."

A knock came at the door. Mace whipped around and saw Aya through the window. She was shaking her head. Mace let her in.

"Why'd you do that?" she scolded. "I was telling you not to."

Shoved from behind, she stumbled forward into Mace's arms. The foam-faced guard they'd knocked out in the hall stood behind her.

He stormed forward, looming over them, trapping them all inside. His stance was unsteady. The foam had been scooped away from his bloodshot eyes. "Back away from the computer," he said.

Mace reached a hand into the zipped-down portion of

his flight suit and said, "Freeze. I have your gun right here. Now back into the corner. Don't make me use it."

"Prove it," the guy said. "You don't have anything ins—"

Out of nowhere, Aya launched herself into the air, feet first, and double drop-kicked the guard square in the chest. He stumbled backward, keeled over, and fell on his side. Aya hit the ground and rolled out of the way.

Just as quickly as Aya had attacked, Dex was somehow across the room, on top of the guy, pressing the crossbar of his chair across the guard's throat.

The guard gasped for breath and uselessly swung his arms as Dex pressed his weight down more fiercely on the chair's choke point. "People on TV always drop like flies and stay down for hours when you hit them on the head," he explained as the others watched, mesmerized. "That's not how it works in real life. You've got to . . . really . . . make them . . . pass out."

The guard's face turned an alarming purple and then he went limp.

"This time, tie him up good. Duct tape. Use the whole roll." Dex rose and carried his chair back to the computer, jamming the memory spike into a port and punching the Enter button.

"There's tape in the assembly room," said Aya. "Be right back."

When she returned, Mace helped her wrap up the stirring guard like a mummy.

"This is weird," said Dex, leaning forward to study the lines of code on the computer screens.

"What is it?" asked Mace.

"I'm not sure yet."

"Hurry up."

"Just give me a second."

The guard was coming around. He gave Mace a glassy-eyed look and started to struggle. Mace double-wrapped his wrists behind his back, just to be safe.

"Guys, I think I'm right about this," said Dex. He was pointing at specific lines of code on the central display and cross-referencing them with additional code on the other displays, reading through them methodically.

"What does that mean?" asked Mace. The guard started to moan, so Mace taped his mouth shut.

"Cover his ears," Dex told them. "Cover his eyes."

Mace and Aya got to work, shoving balls of duct tape in the guard's ears and then pulling his hood down tight. He struggled weakly and gave up, concentrating on breathing through flaring nostrils.

"Thanks. He shouldn't know we know this."

"Know what? What is it, Dex?" Aya barked.

Dex pointed at specific groupings of code on the monitors, each in turn, speaking quietly. "Infinite Dynamic's source code has a back door big enough to drive a submarine through."

"That sounds appropriate," Mace surmised.

"No. It's not. Listen, whoever buys this tech will never be fully in command, not really. Sentinel's built in a Trojan horse! He can always take over, with this subnet here."

"Where?" asked Mace.

"All of this! Here!" Dex was jumping in his seat, growing frustrated as he indicated the whole collection of displays. "The master kill switch will be untraceable once it's off this physical server. But it'll clone itself into every vehicle. Sentinel will always be in charge of the AI fleet."

"So, he could sell this stuff to, Kreznia, let's say, for a bazillion dollars," mused Aya, eyeing Mace narrowly, "and Olesya could send the vehicles into battle . . ."

Dex nodded. "And at any time, if he wanted to, Sentinel

could turn every vehicle around and use them to attack Kreznia himself."

"We have to warn her," Mace stated.

Aya rolled her eyes and glared at him.

"Warn who?" asked Dex.

"The princess," said Aya, a bit smugly. "She's here with her dad right now, on a test drive."

Dex was stunned. "She was behind my kidnapping?"

"I don't know, Dex," said Mace. "But she's going along with it."

Dex's face darkened. "Let her buy it, for all I care. She and her father will get what's coming to them."

"You guys play judge and jury later," insisted Aya. "Let's get out of here alive first, okay?"

Dex yanked the memory wand from the server bank. "I'm done. I've got it all. Whatever your plan is, let's do it."

"Follow me," Mace said.

They scrambled toward the factory floor, stopping twice so Dex could shift the weight of the chair he was hauling, and once to duck into a side room as a pair of unsuspecting techs breezed past. Thanks to Aya, the new prototype Yeti transport morpher was off the assembly conveyor and on solid ground. A spherical robotic fuel hub had been secured in the cargo hold, and the large vehicle was partially fueled and ready to roll.

Simon the deputy fleet technician was on the floor, his feet and his wrists tied together and fastened to a thick pipe, all with duct tape. The boys stared at the man in amazement.

"Did I mention I had already used some of the tape?" Aya asked, smiling.

"You'll never get out of here," Simon warned. "All three of you are insane. And when you're recaptured, there's going to be hell to pay."

Aya ripped off a new piece of duct tape from her trusty roll and used it on the deputy's mouth.

Mace strode over to a control board and started flipping switches. The robotic arms that had built the Yeti began to whip purposefully to and fro.

"Okay, Dex," Mace said. "Everything's on. Time it just right: toss the chair over that beam next time it swings this way, and then duck. The chain will snag on that gear over there, right? The return rotation should snap it no prob, then you can dart out of the way."

251

Dex gave his friend a cold laugh. "And if I *don't* time it just right? That rotation will snap off my *leg*, no prob."

"Listen," argued Mace. "I don't know how to operate all this stuff aside from flipping everything on. We don't have time to experiment. Just heave the chair through next time it cycles back. I'll help."

Dex grumbled something under his breath and crouched on the seat of the chair, steadying himself. He watched the machinery operate, separate parts moving in perfect concert, like a multi-armed conductor leading a particularly complex orchestra. His head bobbed up and down as he got the timing of it. Then he raised his leg, and he and Mace hoisted the chair up and over the beam. There was a crunch. The assembly line machine paused ever so slightly, straining to grind through the metal chains. Then, with a dull snap, the robot arm continued to swing back around. Dex and Mace both ducked and rolled out of the way.

"Oh, hey!" Aya held up a tool from a work bench. "Look, I found bolt cutters."

"What?" cried Dex. "You mean I just did that for nothing?"

Sirens drowned out Dex's protests, ringing from

everywhere. An angry, amplified voice spoke over the noise: "All hands. The prisoners are loose. They're dressed in patrol gear. Stop them."

"Our five minutes are up," Mace declared. "Everyone on the Yeti!" He climbed into the cabin. Aya leaped on board behind him. Dex joined them, slipping on a bundle of patrol gear that Aya had placed on the seat for him.

Mace sat down at the controls, suddenly uncertain. *It's not a race car*, he told himself. *Take the reins; get a feel for her.* Clenching his jaw, he grabbed the wheel. He studied the dash and the console levers for several seconds, fired up the ignition. His feet couldn't find a gas pedal, but there was a throttle by his right hand. He nudged it forward, and they lurched into motion.

Mace's stomach did a flip. *You're fine.*

"Find the clicker," Aya said. "There!" Dex reached for the familiar-looking remote clipped to the visor above him and gave the button a squeeze.

The barn doors rumbled open as the Yeti paraded in wheeled-transport mode along the factory aisle.

A door along the factory's second story opened, and four guards poured onto the catwalk hugging the wall.

They raced in single file toward a steep metal staircase leading down to the factory floor.

"We're about to have company," said Mace.

"Faster," said Aya. She placed her own gloved hand on top of Mace's and shoved the throttle all the way forward. The Yeti accelerated.

"Aya!" cried Mace. The bay doors were still too narrow. He tried pulling back on the throttle.

Aya wouldn't let him. "No time to wait," she stated. "You a TURBOnaut, or what?"

The Yeti barreled through the too-small opening, scraping violently on either side as it punched through to the outdoors while building momentum.

A storm churned beyond the large bay doors. The increased cover was welcome, but Mace already worried that whiteout conditions could complicate takeoff once they reached the trimorphers.

"What's the best way to the east bunker?" asked Mace.

"I have schematics here," Dex announced, plugging the memory spike into a port while still fidgeting with his bulky patrol coat. A dashboard screen came to life and Dex studied it, tapping icons and swiping through various displays.

"The island is shaped like a giant crescent moon," he reported. "We're at the bottom tip. Looks like this small square here is the bunker. Go around this rock spire and head by land straight for the middle of the outside curve."

"Got it," Mace said. He morphed into a snowcat to tackle the deep snow and veered for the middle of the island. The cabin lifted higher and centered over the tank treads and the cargo hold. They now had a 360-degree view of the outside world. Dex shivered and used the sudden extra elbow room to finish donning snow gear.

The going was rough and loose at this speed, but . . .

You a TURBOnaut, or what?

Mace didn't slow down.

Aya pointed behind them. "We're not alone. Where's everyone coming from? The base was so empty."

The boys glanced backward. Just visible through the curtain of snow, framed against the damaged edges of the widening bay doors, more than a dozen snowcats were shifting into forward gear. Mace caught a glimpse of two riderless motorcycles darting through the chaos toward the front line. They morphed into snowmobiles when they got outside.

"That's the AI fleet," he said.

The unmanned snowmobiles flanked the Yeti on either side and rocketed ahead, crisscrossing once and then coming together and slowing, as if to force Mace to stop.

"Keep going!" Aya yelled. She leaned on the throttle again when Mace let off. "Run them over!"

"Plow right over them?" Mace asked.

Baby stroller. White van.

"Yes!" Aya yelled. "We're in a tank."

"All right. Stop grabbing the controls. I'll do it."

Mace gave the snowcat gas and rammed the snowmobiles. They snagged against each other, and the tank's treads caught ahold of one of them. The tank easily rolled over the top of the pair, pressing them down into the deep snow. The cabin jolted violently.

Mace noticed he was still alive. With a hint of a grin, he continued forward at full speed.

This time, four snowmobiles came out of the haze, two on either side of them, and they again took up a position ahead of the tank in hopes of steering Mace awry.

"Keep going," Aya argued.

"There's too many," Mace said.

"You'll crush them, just like last time."

"No," Mace insisted. It wasn't that he was afraid; he was certain of the physics. "We'll flip if we try to take on all four."

In the rearview, two snowcats were gathering speed, a pair of human pilots visible as vague silhouettes within each cabin.

"This isn't going to work," Dex pointed out. "We need time to fuel *Lotus* and *Silverado*. But we're escorting a pack of guards and ghost battering rams right to the trimorphers. We're done for."

Mace was thinking the same thing. He veered away from the line of riderless snowmobiles up ahead, making a beeline for the nearest shore. Maybe they could go submersible. The snowmobiles couldn't follow them underwater.

He looked at his fuel gauge. Very low. That could be a problem.

Or maybe it was an opportunity.

"Dex, can you go into the cargo hold, grab the fuel hose? The Yeti's thirsty."

"What?" said Aya. "We need that fuel for the trimorphers."

"Just a little bit," Mace emphasized. "We don't need to outrun the fleet. We just need to outlast it."

///// CHAPTER TWENTY-THREE

"That might work," Dex admitted. "But how do we refuel without stopping?"

Mace shot him a hopeful look. "That's where you come in."

"Really? You want me to drag a live gas nozzle outside the cabin?"

"You're the cowboy, Caballero." Mace winked. He had reached the water's edge on the western, inside curve of the moon-shaped bay. "Ride the bull."

Dex took a deep breath. "I'll see what I can do." He

lowered his snow mask over his face and looped on some goggles. With a final zip of his patrol jacket, he saluted his friends. "Freaking cold out there, FYI."

The cornice overhanging the lapping shore showed that the snow was at least five feet deep through here. Colonies of penguins huddled together on gravelly beach outcroppings. Mace turned and followed the shore while penguins scattered. He'd morph underwater once Dex was done fueling.

Dex ducked through a small door half against the back wall and half on the floor of the cabin, going down steps to reach the cargo hold.

Aya was on her feet, leaning forward to stare out the window at the nearest snowmobile. "Let me at that console," she told Mace.

"Now what? I'm at full throttle."

"You're driving fine. I have an idea. Those mobiles have external USB ports. Can't we program a kill switch on the memory spike that'll disengage their AI?"

"Go for it," Mace said. Aya worked quickly, tapping through dash displays and accessing a light keyboard.

Dex emerged from belowdecks, uncoiling the gas hose.

"Steady, okay?" he told Mace.

Mace lowered the throttle just a little. He did his best to pick a smooth path over the snow-crusted beach. Visibility only extended fifty feet out, so he had to make adjustments quickly. Dex opened the far cabin door, and a gust of the coldest wind Mace had ever imagined swirled inside. Dex shrieked like he was in an old horror movie. "I've already lost an ear to frostbite!" he complained, lifting the hood of his jacket before stepping out.

Up the slope, the snowmobiles were circling back around, making ready for another try at a blockade. Six driverless snowcats and two piloted ones were in hot pursuit. Another three Jet Skis and four tender boats were on the bay, drawing near through the haze. "Get this over with!" Mace urged.

"I should have offered to drive," Dex muttered, teeth chattering. "But if I die out here, you should know you've always been the better pilot."

"Not now, Dex."

"No, really. I make a better wingman. Exhibit A." He winked and ducked outside the Yeti snowcat. As he sidled along the exterior for several beats, the chain cuffed to his ankle dangled inches from the whipping tread. Dex dipped low to access the gas cap and begin fueling. Mace couldn't watch. He had to study the layout ahead. One wrong bump and Caballero would be bucked off the narrow platform and torn to shreds by the whirring treads.

"There's more in the code," Aya said, "than just what Dex spotted."

"Seriously? What'd you find?"

"It's what I didn't find. It's far worse than we thought. We have to stop the Kreznians from buying into this."

"Why?"

"Done," she suddenly declared. She unplugged the memory spike from the dashboard. "I'll explain later." Aya gave him a wry smile. She flipped up the furry-lined hood on the coat she was wearing. "I've always wanted to try this." She winked.

"Um. Aya? What are you doing?"

She slid behind Mace and opened the driver's-side door, then stepped out on the landing. "Bring me up beside this one." She pointed out the nearest autonomous snowmobile. "Speed up a bit to match its approach."

Not believing what he was seeing, Mace obeyed, veering as he sped up.

"Aya," He shouted out to her. "What if you get hurt?"

"I won't."

"What did you mean—'it's worse than we thought'?"

"Think about it, Mace. This AI has to *learn* before it's good at stuff."

"Right. So?"

"The combat parcels in the master code are blank slates! Where do you think Sentinel plans to teach his baby fleet the art of combat?"

Mace's mind had too much going on. He couldn't concentrate on his thoughts. "Here? Are you saying they let us escape?" The question was too late. Aya was gone.

She'd leaped at just the right moment and landed on the empty snowmobile seat. She fumbled, steadying herself, as the snowmobile continued accelerating and pulling forward in front of the big snowcat. Mace decelerated, worried he could run her over and throw Dex to his death at the same time.

What was she talking about?

He watched with bated breath as Aya retrieved the memory spike from her coat with a gloved hand and lined it up with the USB port. Finally, she fought off the jarring forces and made it fit. Within seconds, she took control of the vehicle. She revved the mobile into higher speed, steering it left, forcing the other snowmobile into a wider path. She snatched back the spike and hopped from the first mobile to the second.

The abandoned mobile stopped in its tracks. Mace rolled over the top of it as Aya veered away.

"Hey!" he heard Dex protest over the wind and the roar of motors.

"Sorry!" Mace called out to him. "That should be enough. Come on back."

Aya dropped beside Mace on her second hijacked snow-mobile. She shouted up to him, "I could take out a few more robots this way, or I could head for the trimorphers and get to work on removing the flash foam and airbag compressor systems behind *Silverado*'s seat. That'd save us some time."

He gave her a thumbs-up. "Sounds good. We'll hit the water and drive these guys in circles until they're out of gas. We'll come find you. Unless we get caught. Then come rescue us again."

"Okay, sure," Aya said. "Right after I win the Prix." She split away, heading up and over a steep hill on her way to the east shore, where the trimorphers were supposed to be stored. Mace slammed his door shut. One of the piloted snowcats broke formation and pursued her. He considered engaging the breakaway soldiers but realized the entire fleet would follow.

Aya was going to have to fend those guys off on her own.

Dex re-entered the cabin and tossed the gas hose back down into the cargo hold. "We got lots of company on the water," he told Mace.

"Gotcha." The fleet was materializing on all sides, by water and by land, tightening into another blockade. A human-piloted cat zagged behind them and morphed into a tender boat, taking to the water's surface.

"We can't enter the water yet," Dex said. "The tender boats and Jet Skis are tracking us too close to shore." Mace saw it too: it was like a moving wall, closing in.

"They know where we want to go. They're learning," said Mace.

"But they won't see this coming." He slammed the brakes, halted, and hit reverse at full throttle. Dex didn't see the move coming, either. He wasn't buckled into his seat, and he smashed into the windshield with a painful cry.

"Bug, meet windshield." Mace laughed.

"Not funny!"

The pursuing fleet continued forward for a moment, and then corrected their trajectories. Some of the tender boats ground into reverse; some of them arced around in tight circles. The Jet Skis executed donuts. The bay, already choppy with storm waves, was suddenly a churning cauldron of foam and machines. The patrolmen on the open water veered wide of the swarm, coordinating with each other using handheld mics.

Mace did a little calculation in his head, borrowed the one, and didn't like the answer he came up with. "Hold on," he called. "Let's try again." He halted and abruptly punched the vehicle forward.

Dex snapped back into his seat, buckling himself. "Thanks for the heads-up this time!"

The morphers spun in the ocean again and banged into each other like bumper boats, too slow to untangle themselves as Mace gunned it for the water.

"Hold your breath," Mace said, and slapped the submariner morph icon on the dash as they made contact with the surf. The tender boat drew near as the copilot lifted a flare gun and pointed it toward the Yeti . . . .

The sub dove below the surface, and the nearest Jet Ski just missed bulleting into the cabin windows as it zoomed overhead. Mace let out a holler of relief.

He felt like he'd just dodged a close call on a TURBO course.

A flare plug ricocheted off the glass. The boys yelped as a shallow crack formed outward from the chipped spot.

"Just a glance," said Mace.

"We're pressurizing okay," Dex added as the crack stopped lengthening. "Should be fine."

Mace continued straight toward the middle of the bay as the tank treads folded inward and a turbine behind them kicked on.

The ocean was calm below the surface, and the water was crystal clear. But the light was poor, and the blue surrounding them turned to an opal darkness farther out. Above them was the massive underbelly of an iceberg. A bluish white against the deepening amethyst background, it hovered like a chandelier over the depths. Fish and a cloud of krill circled it. Penguins swam in a school near the surface, disappearing onto the caves and perches of the iceberg above the water. A seal drew near, curious about them, then lurched at a fish straying from its school. Out away from the berg, the dark underbellies of surface vehicles circled. "They're stalking us."

"We could go deeper, circle around the island," Dex suggested. "Resurface after we lose them."

Deeper? Mace thought, more than a little nervous. He glanced skeptically at the crack on the cabin's outer shell. Best not to push their luck. And the GPS indicator no longer showed their location. "I'll get lost. Let's just park it here under the iceberg while they run down their gas circling."

Dex leaned heavily back in his seat. "Finally, a pit stop."

We have to stop the Kreznians from buying Into this.

"Why does Aya suddenly care about the Vaskos?" Mace asked.

"Huh?"

"When you were outside, Aya said the Infinite Dynamic stuff is worse than we know, but I don't get it." Mace explained that she'd noticed the master code's combat parcels were vacant. "She said the AI has to learn combat, and then asked me where it would do that, like the answer was obvious."

"The Prix?"

Mace shook his head. "Prix's so specific. Every individual on their own. And no weapons involved. How does that teach a machine to coordinate in battle?"

"*Academy* had to learn, too," Dex pointed out. "Aya was able to beat Hightower a couple times early on. Remember?"

Mace thought back to the races after London. The matchups that Aya had won had been cross-country competitions, over open, nonrepeating terrain. But as long as *Academy* was doing the same loops over and over again in closed-course terrains, it could learn to improve its technique enough within the time of the race to take the lead and keep it. "But *Academy* did win London," Mace noted. "It didn't start off with empty coding."

"Well, it obviously practiced somewhere."

Mace shot up, cradling his forehead in astonishment. "That's it! That's why they never found a body!"

"Yo, man. You're freakin' me out."

"There was a wrecked-out morpher by the cliffs near Punta Arenas," Mace explained.

No corpse had ever turned up after Juan Pablo Garcia's fiery street race. No one had ever seen the pilot eject, either.

Yet the seat was gone, leading everyone to assume they'd missed something in the dark.

But what if that vehicle had never had a pilot? Or a seat?

Mace continued, "This guy, Juan Pablo, he raced a mysterious morpher in Punta Arenas. He told me everything went south when the other guy tried to avoid hitting a tumbleweed."

No drone pilot would care about a tumbleweed in its path. But a robot intelligence, on its first live test run against its first real human opponent—might mistake a tumbleweed for a dangerous obstacle. And try to avoid hitting it.

"It was a test vehicle," Mace said. He let the words hang in the chilly cabin. "It was a prototype for *I'd Like to Thank the Academy*."

"Oh, I get what Aya was on about now." Dex nodded. "Kreznia."

Mace thought for a second, then he caught on, too. "Their civil war . . . Sentinel plans to use their battlefield as a *test run*."

"A test run for what?" asked Dex.

A chill ran down Mace's back. He imagined the tumbleweed . . . the fiery crash. "Does that matter at this point?

The Vaskos are about to spend their nation's fortune on an army with zero real-world experience. They'll be crushed— just like when the prototype TURBO racer choked when it encountered an unexpected tumbleweed. But Sentinel will download all the data—use that war zone to train his machines for when he wants to use them for his own purposes later. He wins no matter what."

Dex's expression darkened as he caught on. "We need to warn Olesya."

"Try getting her on the comm," Mace told him.

Dex nodded and started testing frequencies. "Olesya? Princess Vasko? Come in. It's Dex. And Mace is here too. We know you're in Antarctica."

They repeated the search around the dial. Finally, her voice crackled on the speakers. "Mace? Dex? How are you reaching me?"

"We're stuck on this island!" shouted Mace. "Who do you think the fleet is chasing around?"

"I don't know what's going on," she told the boys. "Father and I were ordered back to the base suddenly."

"That's because we're here. We're trying to escape, but Sentinel has other plans."

"What?" The princess sounded genuinely confused. "You guys need to stay out of this. What about the Prix?"

"We were kidnapped, Olesya!" cried Dex. "We're trying to get away!"

"Olesya, listen to me," Mace pleaded. "You can't do this deal with Sentinel. We've seen the code. He's using you."

"We're doing it for independence, Mace. We have every right to demand back what's rightfully ours. I'm sorry all of you got caught up in this. I didn't want any of you involved. I asked Hightower yesterday if he'd done something with Dex. He said no, but I guess he was lying—"

"I don't care about that!" Mace barked. "I mean, I do! But you definitely shouldn't be doing business with Infinite Dynamic!"

The princess shared a rueful sigh. "My father's mind is made up."

A new voice rang out. "Cut your mic, Olesya." It was Sentinel. "Don't listen to them."

"Mace! Watch out!" cried Dex, bolting upright. He motioned out the window.

In the deep just beyond the iceberg, a submersible spiraled down toward them, hugging close to the ice. The glass-domed cabin was lit from within. Sentinel was centered like a giant, luminous cat's-eye pupil emerging from the dark.

The pod drew near, propelled by a single-prop turbine. Sentinel's craft extended spidery legs, reaching out to seize Mace and Dex.

CHAPTER TWENTY-FOUR /////

The determination on Sentinel's face filled Mace with terror. Mace plunged the vehicle downward and swooped left—but not quickly enough to avoid the reach of a spidery tentacle on the commander's submersible. A claw at its end scraped the Yeti's hull—then gripped it tight. Both vehicles lurched off trajectory and snapped into a spin like square-dance partners.

"Shake him, Mace!" cried Dex. "He'll claw his way back to shore and drag us with him."

"Working on it," Mace muttered. He fully reversed the throttle and initiated a barrel roll. The other morpher's grasp never faltered. "Look around. Do we have robotic arms too? An external cutting tool?"

"I don't see anything like that," Dex yelled. "We're in a transport, not a Swiss Army knife."

"That's it! I got it! Make every morph matter!"

"Mace! No! We're too deep! You don't know if there's—"

Thirty feet beneath the icy Antarctic bay, Mace flipped a dashboard switch, and the Yeti began its conversion from a sub to a wheeled transport.

Transformer modules cranked into gear. The shape of the cabin shifted. From every direction at once, water sprayed and gushed into the cabin from countless parting seams. Mace and Dex screamed involuntarily as colder-than-ice saltwater doused them.

But it worked! The spider arm was severed along the path of two rotating exterior panels. The Yeti, taking on water, sank quickly out of the commander's reach. Walls of water battered Mace and Dex from all sides as the transport slow-tumbled toward the bay floor.

Pushing against what felt like a fire hose, Mace struggled forward in his seat, gasping for breath, and morphed their sinking sarcophagus back into a sub. The seams in the walls and floor closed. Soaked and breathless, Mace gathered his bearings, gripped the wheel with frozen hands, and propelled the submersible back into motion toward the shore. The joints in his fingers throbbed with icy pain, but he maintained steady control of the steering.

Sentinel retracted the spidery tentacles and gave chase, but the Yeti was now comfortably beyond reach.

Mace shuddered. "Rinse cycle complete," he said.

Dex was shivering uncontrollably. "You're out of your mind." His teeth chattered as he fumbled with the hot air.

"Mace, what's happening?" Princess Vasko's voice crackled through the Yeti's speakers.

The two fugitives shared a look. Dex turned up the volume on the comm. Mace hesitated, then answered. "I'm trying to warn you. Sentinel's using your war to teach his AI how to fight. Then he'll take his fleet back and use it somewhere else for his own purposes."

He throttled up and began to rise. Sentinel pursued in radio silence. Mace slingshotted wide before surfacing, where the iceberg was thickest around, hoping to stay beyond Sentinel's line of sight. But the water was too clear. Numerous unmanned crafts tracked their movements in tight formation on the surface above.

He made landfall at full speed, punching through a shrinking hole in the formation of surface vehicles. Mace's Yeti morphed back into a snowcat, and the AI vehicles copied, but Mace was in the lead. He barreled straight up a steep slope. One of the AI craft chose to tackle a giant outcropping of rock along its path by morphing into spider form, instead of veering around it. A mistake. The crawlers were no match against the snowcats, and Mace gained a significant lead by the time the AI vehicle morphed back into a tread runner.

Mace grew distantly aware at first, and then with more focus, that he hadn't felt fear at the helm since they'd shot out of the facility. The speed, the danger, the risk: he'd shoved all of it aside in the name of reaching escape velocity.

That natural confidence—that singular lack of hesitation—*he'd gotten it back.*

"Commander, do you want us to engage?" a new voice asked over the airwaves.

"No. Stand down. Let the AI units proceed. They're learning. Just send someone to get the stranded men in the bay." Sentinel sounded strained, furious.

"Copy that. Alpha base out," the other voice replied.

Mace shot Dex a skeptical look. He clicked the comm. "Did you hear that, Olesya? These things are nowhere close to combat ready. He still has to train them—in *your* war zone."

The cabin had grown warm, and though the boys were still pretty wet, at least they weren't about to freeze into meat popsicles. Mace's spirits rose as his shivering ceased. There was a break in the storm and visibility improved. The clouds whipped by, low and thick, but they had parted enough that the snow flurries stopped. Mace could see that the top of the hill was within reach, but he took a sharp turn to avoid cresting it. He had no idea how far the shore would be, or if Aya and the trimorphers would be obvious on the landscape, and he figured it was best to play it safe for now, to continue to wear the fleet down from this side of the island, as they'd been doing all along.

The strategy was paying off. Two more snowcats and the last riderless snowmobile ran out of gas. Sentinel was giving chase, but he had to maneuver through the obstacles of stalled vehicles, which cost him time.

"Olesya," Mace tried yet again. "Sentinel's playing you for fools. He trains his fleet using you, then he'll call them home with a back-door override. He—"

"It's no use, Mace," spat Sentinel's voice across the airwaves. "I jammed their transmissions. The Kreznians can't hear you."

"How can you think you'll get away with this?" Mace demanded.

"I know what you're doing, Mace," Sentinel said. "You're running us out of gas. But it's not going to get you anywhere."

"You're the one at the end of the line," said Mace. "We're stopping you."

"You should know that your friend Aya has already been apprehended," answered Sentinel. "Her break for the east bunker was an obvious move."

Dex and Mace shared a look of devastation. Mace shut off the comm. "Don't listen to him," he told Dex. "He's bluffing."

"No, he's not. Look." Dex pointed out the window, his face crestfallen.

Mace glanced over and saw a plume of smoke rising over a ridge to the east. His heart sank. He almost cut the motor right then and there. What was the point of continuing this chase? They weren't going anywhere without Aya.

Mace hit the comm. "She better not be hurt!"

"Well, that will depend on your next move."

Another snowcat ground to a halt as the chase proceeded along the bay side of the ridge. But the smoke coming over the horizon wrenched at Mace's gut. Was this over? Should they give up or keep going? Aya might be recaptured, but . . . what they now knew *had* to be revealed to the world. She'd want them to go on if they could.

"We have to keep trying," he said to Dex. "If none of us escapes to sound the alarm—all three of us will be stuck here."

"Maybe we can still get her back," Dex said. "We have lots of gas. We have a freaking military-grade morpher at our disposal. We can go back in the water. Hide for a while."

The last unmanned snowcat stuttered and died. All that remained behind them was Sentinel. Maybe Dex's plan wasn't so crazy. "Let's give it a shot," Mace said. "Stay on your toes."

"My toes are frozen." Dex sighed. "I'll stay on my hooves."

"How are you at hand-to-hand combat?" Mace asked.

Dex laughed. "Not as good as Aya—but I've gotten myself out of plenty of scrapes."

They veered, pointed toward the smoke column, and

crested the ridge. The storm dissipated on the east slope, and their view was clear all the way across the open water to the next island.

The commander was doing a good job of staying on their tail but wasn't gaining.

Dex jumped up. "Hey, look!"

The plume of smoke belonged to the charred remains of a snowcat, not a snowmobile. Mace's mouth fell open. A little farther along, the two patrol scouts who had broken off to pursue Aya were struggling across the deep snow on snowshoes.

On a distant rocky beach, Aya's snowmobile was parked beside two trimorphers half-emerged from the open garage door of a snow-covered bunker.

The boys laughed. "What in the world did she do to them?"

"Look at that. She's ready to go!"

Dex crushed Mace's shoulder with a hopeful squeeze. "We still need time to fuel. How are we going to—"

"Shh!" Mace heard a now-familiar sputter cut through the cabin. He felt it, too. "I don't believe it," he cried. "*We're out of gas!*"

"What? I gave it some! I did!" argued Dex.

Mace gritted his teeth. "The tentacle must have nicked the line. Hold on. Let me try something."

Mace morphed the snowcat into a tender boat.

Suddenly fueled by gravity, the tender boat had just enough momentum left on the downhill slope to start gathering speed. The boys cheered, but Sentinel was right behind them. He reached out with the front tentacle again, trying to seize the Yeti, but the tentacle's claw was missing. Eluding the disabled crawler's grasp, the escapees sledded down the hill at top speed.

Sentinel's cat, on the other hand, suddenly shuddered, jerked to the side, and stopped.

"He's out," guessed Dex.

Mace squeezed the wheel to calm his excited shaking. "Finally, something's going our way."

The commander tried to morph into a boat, too, but the angle was wrong. His cabin teetered and then tipped onto its side.

Sentinel angrily called out on the radio. "All personnel to the east bunker, STAT! Belay all previous orders. Suit up. Lock and load!"

"Clock's ticking," Dex muttered through gritted teeth. "Get to the beach."

The makeshift sleigh-version Yeti slowed to a halt on the gravelly landing beside the bunker. Mace and Dex sprang to action beside the two trimorphers parked in front of the bunker. Aya waved at them as she tossed safety equipment out of Dex's cockpit. Penguins stood in loose groups and watched them curiously from rocky outcroppings and snow-covered hunks of ice drifting along the shore.

Dex jumped out of the back of the cargo hold with the long fuel hose and yanked it toward *Silverado*, shoving the nozzle into the trimorpher. He had to step over the discarded safety foam and air compressor system of *Silverado* piled between the crafts. "Just finished tearing these out," Aya explained, hopping to the ground.

"Why'd you take out *mine*?" complained Dex.

Aya shrugged. "I'm not gutting my safety equipment! She's a dicer!"

"That's just awesome," Dex said.

"We don't have a second to spare," said Mace nervously, staring up the side of the steep hill. Sentinel was coming for them on foot, struggling to descend the slope through the deep snow, but making slow progress on snowshoes. He wore a bulky camo backpack.

"What did you do?" Dex asked Aya. "Sentinel told us you were captured."

"I *was* captured," she answered. "But I found a flare gun inside the snowcat. I used it."

"You mean you—you used it? Inside the cabin?" Mace stammered.

Aya nodded cheerfully. "That got their attention. By the time they'd put themselves out, I'd hopped back on my trusty snowmobile."

Mace released a single incredulous bark of laughter. "How'd you get into the bunker, though?"

"Flare gun again! Crawled through the hole, unlocked things from the inside."

Mace looked where she was pointing. The garage door was up, but Mace could see a crispy-edged, still-smoldering hole where the lock should be. "Oh, yeah. Of course," he said.

"Done here," Dex announced. He jumped down from the hull of *Silverado* and they helped him drag the heavy hose over to *Lotus*.

The sound of approaching machines carried to Mace's

283

trained ears. "We better hurry!"

"I'm going as fast as I can!" Dex shouted.

Aya turned to Mace. "You and Dex should take off."

"No," said Mace emphatically. "We go together."

"Load up, at least!" Aya yelled. "Get ready!"

Mace nodded at that. He came up beside *Silverado* and gave the hull an affectionate stroke. Back into a morpher with zero safety equipment. His stomach fluttered, but only a little. He slid into *Silverado*'s rear, and the ball of lead in his gut hovered in place. *It's nothing compared to what you've already done.*

That was true: despite the risk and the amount of concentration and quick thinking it had taken, Mace had fended off an entire robot horde today.

The fleet of vehicles from the upper base came over the far hill in a swarm, growing loud on the quiet air. No baby robot learners this time. A pack of trained and fully armed soldiers barreled down on them.

"You drive," Dex invited him. "I'll take nav."

"No, dude. She's your ride."

Dex shrugged. "She's built exactly the same as *Trailblazer*. You're the 'naut. I'm better off at your side."

"Don't argue. We've gotta go."

"Fine."

As Dex slipped in and gripped the wheel, Mace saw Sentinel stop and retrieve something from his backpack. The sinister motion sent a chill down Mace's back. The commander pointed something at them. A flare rocketed toward them. It fell in the snow and died only twenty feet shy of the fuel tank. The penguins got the message. They sprang into motion, calling out in alarm, bolting for the water in large flocks.

"He's trying to blow us up!" Mace observed.

"And he's going to succeed if he gets much closer," Aya warned.

All three of them watched in growing alarm as Sentinel took large steps through the deep snow.

"Done!" said Aya, dropping the fuel nozzle. "Let's go!" She boarded *Lotus*.

Sentinel raised the flare gun again, steadied his arm. He was aiming right for the fuel tank, and he was close enough now that the flare would reach it.

"STOP!" the commander screamed. "I'll do it. *You know I will!* Get out and come toward me or I blow it all to hell!"

Mace and the others looked everywhere, assessing their

chances. Mace was afraid it was over. Aya must have figured the same thing. She rose out of *Lotus*'s cockpit. "Go," she told him and Dex. "Get out of here. Get the info home. I'll stall him."

"No, Aya. We're not leaving you."

"Do it! Warn everyone!"

"ALL OF YOU! NOW!"

Dex growled but closed the canopy. *Silverado* churned awake. Mace's chest burst with nervous excitement.

But it was too late. The approaching snowcats arrived, crowding around. At the same moment, an AI submersible surfaced on the beach in front of Dex and Mace, blocking them.

"We're screwed," Dex warned. "I told you—you should have taken the wheel."

The boys hopped to the ground with their hands in the air. Mace's stomach was churning with disappointment. He glanced around in a daze as soldiers closed in with weapons drawn.

Mace, Aya, and Dex were taken into custody, their escape plans utterly dashed.

CHAPTER TWENTY-FIVE /////,

Mace was in zero danger of freezing, given that he was chained to a radiator. In fact, he felt uncomfortably warm on one side, and sat flat against the wall as far away from the heating unit as the cuffs and his outstretched arm would allow. His butt was cold, but he couldn't really feel that on account of how numb his entire lower half was. He'd been trapped for hours in the same position. It was nighttime. It was completely dark. He cursed himself for being so uncomfortable that he couldn't fall asleep.

No one else was getting any shut-eye either, apparently.

"I'm freezing," called out Dex from a far corner of the room. "I could *really* use a blanket."

"I'll trade you spots," Mace said into the dark.

"You've got the radiator! What do you have to complain about?"

"Half of me's roasting. The other half's a popsicle. That's what."

From another direction, Aya grumbled. "Shut up, you two. I'm trying to sleep. It's hard enough without all the yammering."

"At least you have a seat cushion," Dex mumbled.

"I will gag all three of you if you wake me up again," inserted another voice altogether, from the couch in the center of the shared space. The voice belonged to the guy Mace had foamed and subsequently mummified in duct tape earlier in the day. Not surprisingly, he hadn't been willing to accommodate many of their requests.

Sentinel wasn't taking any chances. He'd left hours ago, to be at the Prix when it started in the morning. He had personally handcuffed each of the youths to an immovable part of the wall in the common room beside the airport hangar.

Then he'd stationed a full-time guard in the room, and two additional guards posted outside the door, to keep a constant eye on them. "We'll come up with something more permanent when I get back," the commander had explained, tapping an open palm with the memory spike he'd retrieved from Aya's jacket pocket. "But frankly, you deserve to sit here and rot."

Mace gave his cuffed arm a shake to keep it from falling asleep. He'd given up on escape. No more visions of dashing off to freedom through daring heroics. The only thing looping through his head now was a building sense of doom. He had no idea what the future would hold, but he had plenty of cause for worry. The three of them knew far too much about Sentinel's plans.

The guarded door leading into the hallway opened, flooding the common room with light. The soldier on the couch sat up, perturbed. He shielded his eyes as he addressed the approaching silhouette. "What is it now? Why can't I get any—"

Mace heard a thunk. The soldier slumped. The silhouetted figure fell on him with purpose. Mace could smell chloroform from where he sat watching. In the mostly dark, the sound of duct tape being unrolled echoed through the room.

A few seconds later, the lights came on and Princess Vasko stood in the doorway. She wore her wintry uniform and furry Baltic snow hat. She also wore light makeup and polished black boots. She made the whole getup look incredibly trendy—like breaking out of an Antarctic prison was what all the cool kids were doing. Mace's eyes were glued to her.

She scanned the room, pausing to look at each of them. "Speechless?" she asked.

"No," said Aya, sitting cross-legged on a fabric seat cushion with one wrist cuffed to a metal pipe running along the wall. "Just figuring out how to punch you in the face from here."

"I've come to get you out of here," Olesya explained, fishing through the unconscious guard's pockets, "so don't you start."

"What do you expect?" spat Aya. "A thank-you? For so generously allowing us to escape our kidnapping? Oh, thank you, your highness, how can we ever repay you?"

"Aya, shut up and let her do whatever she's going to do," insisted Dex.

"What *are* you going to do?" Mace asked.

"Listen," she started, raising her hand to show off the handcuff key she'd found, "I heard you, Mace—what you were saying about Sentinel using us. You have to understand: my people are very desperate and short on time. My father wants to send a strong signal."

"It's a huge mistake," said Mace. "Sentinel is using *your* conflict to train *his* army. Your country will be giving all the benefits to someone else."

"Kreznia shouldn't be *fighting* to solve its problems, anyway!" Aya spat. "Grow up!"

"My father won't listen. I couldn't stop him. But you can." She smugly passed by Aya and came over to Mace first and freed him from the radiator.

He stood up on weak legs and rubbed his sore wrist. "What do you mean?"

"I got him to compromise. It's the only thing both he and Sentinel would agree to. Sentinel laughed when I suggested it. He agreed right away. I don't think he dreamed I'd come back here and get you."

"What's the compromise?" asked Dex, as Olesya freed him. He used the key to finally uncuff his ankle from its broken chain. He ran straight to the kitchen area and started rifling through the fridge.

Olesya cleared her throat and gave all three TURBOnauts a wry smile. "If *I'd Like to Thank the Academy* doesn't win the Glove, the deal is off."

"Well, that's a dumb bet," Dex told her as he returned, his mouth full of someone else's leftover peanut butter sandwich. "*Academy* hasn't lost a race except to Aya. No one else racing in the Prix has a prayer of taking *Academy* down."

"You think I don't know that?" said Olesya, unlocking Aya's cuffs. "That's why I'm here. There's still time. *Lotus* and *Silverado* are both registered to race. If we get them to the starting line before the green flag drops, it's all legit."

"We should just go back and tell the authorities what we know," insisted Aya. "Let them sort it out."

"Which authorities?" asked Olesya. "You heard Sentinel, he has all sorts of top secret clearances for this. There's only one way: make sure *Academy* loses tomorrow."

"Olesya," said Dex, shaking his head. "I'm not going to

beat *Academy*. I can't. I know that. There's too much on the line for me not to be totally honest about it."

"I'll try," Aya stated.

Everyone looked at her as if she'd just given them all whiplash.

She shrugged. "What Olesya said made sense. And if there's still time for me to race in the Prix in the morning, I'm going to do it anyway! I worked too hard all year for the Glove. We have to try. And this is a variable-terrain race, so *Academy* can't just get it perfect through repetition. We have a shot at this!"

"I don't know," said Dex.

"If you won't pilot *Silverado*," argued Aya, "Mace should. The more of us in the race, the better our odds of beating *Academy*."

Dex perked up. "Great idea. Mace: you do it. Put on my helmet and win me the Glove!"

"Are you guys crazy?" Mace demanded, reaching for some of the food Dex was transferring to the counter. "You know how rusty I am? How out of shape I still might be?" A flutter of nervousness shot through him at the mere thought. "I haven't done any run-throughs. I haven't studied the route. Dex, you're in a far better position to compete than me."

Dex shook his head and dropped a heavy hand on Mace's shoulder. "No, dude. I've taken on that AI ten times this season. I never get close. It has to be you. You can study the route on the way back."

Olesya clapped her hands together. "Don't you see, Mace? You're the only one who hasn't raced the AI yet. You're better for this situation. Dex has raced the AI and lost. Aya's beaten the AI, but that only means she's taught it a thing or two. *Academy* thinks it knows how to handle *Silverado*, but it won't see this coming."

The guard on the couch stirred. He tried to sit up, realized he was tied up in duct tape, and fell back. "Not again!" he moaned.

Olesya pressed the chloroform rag to his face again, and he grew still. "Whatever we do, we're running out of time. We have to go. I say Mace takes the wheel. Aya, you and Mace fly your morphers straight to the starting gate. I saw them both in the hangar as I came in. Looks like Sentinel was planning to keep them and modify them. I'll take Dex back with me in my jet. Much faster than a morpher, and we don't have to refuel along the way. We'll get back sooner and set everything up, so your crews are stationed and ready by morning."

"You fly a jet?" Dex asked her incredulously.

"It comes with a pilot," she assured them.

Mace released a deep sigh. "This could actually work," he admitted. "The AI doesn't know me. And Aya's right: we have to try."

"So how do we keep these guys from radioing ahead?" asked Dex, pointing at the guard on the couch, and two pairs of legs visible in the hall. "They'll warn Sentinel, and he'll stop us from racing."

"No, he won't," said Olesya. "Sentinel will know that if he interferes, we'll just return the favor and tell Gimbal *Academy* is AI. She'll yank Hightower from the race in a heartbeat. Besides: he wants to win the Glove. He'll let this play out."

"I don't know." Aya hesitated. "We should be sure. Just in case, can we toss these guards in the jet to keep an eye on them? The race starts in five hours. By the time anyone else around here wises up, it'll be too late."

"Let's do it," Mace said. "Let's roll!"

The four of them shared a high five and helped one another drag all three squirming, groggy guards, bound in their duct tape, over to Olesya's Kreznian jet, where her private pilot helped to secure them on board.

"Call my parents right away," Aya told Olesya. "Tell them I'll call as soon as I can."

"Done," said Olesya. "What about you guys?"

"I'm sure my sister's worried," said Dex. "I'll call her in the air."

Mace thought about it. "My parents are unplugged in the Rockies. I'm due for a check-in, but they might not have any news. I'll email them when we land."

A few minutes later, *Silverado* and *Lotus* morphed together to air and took to the clear starry sky, bulleting north. Mace felt surprisingly at ease behind the controls. Dex had been right: with the exception of her gutted safety features and paint job, *Silverado* was a perfect clone of *Trailblazer*. Mace gave the dash a tender touch, feeling what she had on the inside. She hummed just like *Trailblazer*, too. Mace smiled. Dex was a gifted engineer.

"Are you going to race?" Mace asked himself.

He knew the answer was yes. *I have to.*

Mace flew beside Aya over the Drake Passage, even though her dicer had a slower top speed. This allowed them to keep an eye on each other in case trouble arose.

A while later, running on fumes, they dove beneath an angry sea. Aya led the way, using the coordinates she'd uploaded earlier to pinpoint the location of the hidden fueling station.

Lotus and *Silverado* shot back out of the water and dashed side by side north, toward South America and a bruised horizon promising daylight and a new beginning.

///// CHAPTER TWENTY-SIX

Mace glanced around at the pink snowcapped hilltops. They were on their final approach to Punta Arenas, coming in low just a few feet above the water along a channel between the islands of the Tierra del Fuego. It was dawn. The start of the Gauntlet Prix was minutes away. "You go in first," Mace suggested. "We shouldn't be seen arriving out of nowhere together."

"Good thinking," answered Aya. "Make every morph matter."

"I guess it's time we cut the comm. Crosstalk is illegal

during the race. But we've got this. Together we can do this. If I have to, I'll run interference for—"

"No, Mace," Aya interjected pointedly.

"Huh? Did I say something wrong?"

"No. But . . . yes." Aya drew in a deep breath. "We're not together anymore. There's no we."

Mace felt hurt. He wasn't sure what he'd done. They'd both been awake for forever—maybe one or both of them was getting loopy.

"I want that Glove, and I want it fair and square. I've worked really hard for two years to get it. When I win today, I don't want to have any doubts about why. You can take your chivalrous do-goodery and shove it. If you're a real TURBOnaut, then you'll try to crush me out there— always."

Mace was silent as he let her words sink in. She was right, of course: starting now, they weren't friends anymore. They were rivals. Beating the AI racer was essential so that Olesya's father could honorably walk away from the agreement he'd already committed to with Sentinel. But today's race was about more than just that. It was about being the best.

Aya's grit and determination awoke within Mace a dormant hunger: *this is the Gauntlet Prix. This is TURBO Racing. I'm back. I want this.*

There'll always be an asterisk next to your name, Renegade. . . .

Mace felt a surge of adrenaline. He remembered what that felt like: not to win, but to *want* to win. To want to win so badly you couldn't sit still.

"You got it, sister," Mace told her finally. "See you on the podium below me. Over and out."

He shut off the comm and watched *Lotus* bank heavily to the left and vanish over the hills along another sea channel.

Mace circled low in the valley then touched down near the morpher warehouse. The relief he felt at being back in the real world was immense. He parked *Silverado* in its team stall and was met immediately by Dex and Olesya.

"Bathroom break," Mace stated. "And parents."

His crew chief nodded. "Be quick. You should already be lining up on the track. We'll get you fresh parts and fuel and a diagnostic check."

Olesya stopped him and forced a hug on him. "I'll leave you alone," she said, "but I'll be watching everything with my father from the sky box. Good luck out there."

"Beating *Academy* isn't enough, you know," Mace told her. "It only buys us time. You have to convince your dad to drop this altogether. And then we still have to stop Sentinel from selling his war machines to someone else."

"I know," she replied. "But one thing at a time. If *Academy* loses, he'll listen to reason. Now, go out there and kick Rad Thad's butt."

Mace led himself into Caballero's private locker room, where he changed into a fresh *Silverado* flight suit. On the computer at the workstation, he scrolled through emails from people wondering where he was. His parents had reminded him to check in, but they didn't seem alarmed. Mace shuddered, realizing that if they hadn't escaped, his whereabouts would have remained a complete mystery to everyone. He messaged them immediately:

I'm back in Punta Arenas after a crazy few days. No idea what the news is saying, but know that I'm safe. I'll explain what happened later. Right now, I need you guys to drop everything and watch the Prix. I'll be racing *Silverado*!

This is nuts, he thought. His stomach churned. He wasn't sure how any of this was going to play out.

"I'll know in a few," he told the quiet workshop, rubbing his exhausted eyes. With a deep sigh, he hopped into his tri-morpher, donned a generic black helmet, and rolled out to the track.

A couple minutes later, *Silverado* was situated on the starting line, idling next to *I'd Like to Thank the Academy* and behind *Lotus* and *Untouchable.*

Dex came up beside the vehicle. The canopy lifted. They fist-bumped each other. "Make every morph matter," Dex said.

"Hey, I didn't remember to look before I leaped inside: did you have time to replace the safety equipment behind me?"

The question was met with silence.

"Dex?"

"I'm not going to answer that," he finally answered. "But you probably shouldn't crash today."

Fabulous, Mace thought. His stomach filled with lead. *Just what I need.*

"We got ahold of JP. Great suggestion. His uncle halted

the missing-persons investigations. And he and his cousin agreed to crew the remote pit stops. They know it's you behind the wheel, but none of the other *Silverado* crew do."

"Good. We need a lid on this until it's over."

"We've got you covered."

Engines roared.

Dex barked into Mace's ear, "Punch the ignition!"

Mace groaned. He dropped the canopy and did what he was told.

The purr of the machine calmed him. His hands were steady. He flexed his gloves as he gripped the wheel. *Silverado* felt like a glove itself, bending itself to Mace's fingers. Mace had only to command, and the trimorpher would do his bidding.

The green flag waved. The four leaders sprang off the line. A herd of followers crowded Mace's rearview, but he paid the others no heed. No looking back. The next several hours were about moving forward. As fast as physics would allow. And nothing else.

Mace was still in fourth when he executed the early morph to water, but he muscled his way up through the leaders with an urgency that suggested the finish could come any second, not several hours from now. The effort paid off. He came out of the channel and took to the long stretch of rough highway in second place, behind only *Academy*, ahead of Aya by a smidge. And he stayed there, riding *Academy*'s tail for a comfortable fifty miles, while *Lotus* rode his. No mistakes. He drifted with better precision than the AI, feeling the imperfections in the road, anticipating every course correction better. This was how he would win. On the ground. On these roads. The wide, sweeping curves around snowcapped mountains, the smaller zigzags around exposed crags and rocks, pavement cracked and buckled from the constant freeze-thaw of the bottom of the continent. Mace was one with *Silverado* as she fit to the curves and angles tighter than the golden coat of paint on *Academy*. Even the smears of ice and drifts of snow that clung to the turns felt oddly familiar, after Mace's run for freedom over the Antarctic landscape.

The AI could calculate faster. It knew how to adapt. But Mace could *feel* everything. He knew how to anticipate.

Mace downshifted, hugging the curve in the road tighter than usual for a race this long. But he needed to shave every millisecond he could off his run if he was going to best the leader.

The race sped on and on.

"*Untouchable* is right behind you," Dex reported. "Aya's right behind her."

Untouchable's Akshara Brahama: she was young, herself—just old enough to race without controversy. She'd placed last year, too. Mace was certain she was thirsty for the outright win today.

The strange, gangly trees on the steep, upslope side of the course stretched into vague lines, in stark contrast to the unchanging ocean channel far beneath the cliffs to Mace's left. He'd landed and bolted in roadster form through the town of Cabo de Hornos, dropping back briefly to sixth place. But now he screamed west, doubling back toward Ushuaia on their winding route to the halfway mark after having passed Aya and Akshara, *Flipside, Guillotine, Paradox*, and *Velocity Raptor*.

Mace regained second. He was feeling pretty good holding there after such a grueling slog through most of Tierra del Fuego. But coming in number two was never enough, and especially not today.

Academy, with Hightower on board, launched off a ramp placed at a sharp bend in the road. The trimorpher transformed into a submarine and dove like a bomb toward the sea. The five-mile stretch across the Beagle Channel would continue with a run in the bay of Ushuaia, lined with underwater spectator pods.

Mace counted the seconds before he reached the ramp himself.

One, two, morph.

Plummet.

The weightlessness in Mace's gut went beyond phys-ics. He was terrified. The surface of the water came at him like a—

White van! I have no safety gear on board!

He didn't fight the panic. He acknowledged it—and moved through it to something more like exhilaration. He let the iron core in his gut churn and liquefy into joy.

Mace hit the water like an Olympic diver and arced beau-tifully into a horizontal torpedo. He gunned it for *Academy*.

He caught up enough to take advantage of the lead-er's wake. His flight through the water stabilized, and he increased his gains. Mace didn't wait to execute the sling-shot maneuver around Hightower. He dove, belly-rolled, and came up level and side by side with *Academy*'s nose.

"Caught you!" Mace cried triumphantly.

Academy actually slowed, but Mace wasn't taking the bait. "Nice try, AI, but I'm not letting you get in my wake for a last-second slingshot of your own."

"Good thinking." Dex spoke in Mace's ears. "You're doing great. Stay right where you are. For now. *Untouchable* and *Lotus* are riding your combined wake. *Velocity Raptor*'s within striking distance. Careful he doesn't try something of his own."

Mace matched *Academy*'s speed. Sensing that its gambit was a waste of time, *Academy* accelerated again. Mace stayed with his rival, with no interest in falling back himself. His fuel was good; his trajectory coming into the hoop checkpoint was ideal. All he had to do was stay fast and inch ahead. Mace glanced over at Hightower. The actor's vague silhouette was stretching his arms while *Academy* did all the work.

Mace flipped him a choice gesture. He let it hang there long enough that Hightower was sure to catch it.

They passed through the next checkpoint side by side. Mace had wondered if the craft would try something near the hoop, but it had remained steady. It was the right decision. He bit his lip; the AI was showing great patience today. It had learned so much about how to maximize endurance. Beating it was going to be tricky. Mace couldn't let his guard down.

Suddenly, *Academy* found a boost of speed. "No, you don't!" Mace matched the machine inch for inch, but *Academy* still had more acceleration in reserve. It was going to pull ahead.

He gave *Silverado* all he had, but it wasn't enough.

Seeing no other option, Mace nudged over, drawing dangerously close to *I'd Like to Thank the Academy*. The rival vehicle didn't push back, knowing that Mace could roll at that point and win ground. It wouldn't be much, but it might be enough to cost *Academy* in the long run. Mace nudged over again. The AI responded by ceding more of the center lane.

Mace smiled. It was treating him like he was gunning for the Glove, all or nothing, in the next ten seconds. It was calculating the best course of action accordingly: let Mace push it wider and wider until it could suddenly, and at the last second, swoop low and around and win back the center, boosted by Mace's wake.

Aya took advantage. She shot ahead, duking it out for

bragging rights at the halfway point. But the lead now didn't amount to squat. *Academy* executed a last-second maneuver against Mace that won it half an inch of leeway coming into Ushuaia. Mace had considered the risk of this and had been willing to make the sacrifice.

Over the next hour, Mace lost ground to Aya. But *Untouchable* fell even farther back, conceding fifth to *Paradox* and *Velocity Raptor.* The end felt near. They left the water and morphed straight to air, rising quickly up and over a steep, snow-covered mountain to battle it out over the treetops of the next valley. Aya and the other dicers took a different route through the low, forested hills. Mace concentrated on keeping up with *Academy*'s air tactics. He toyed with the AI, darting forward and backward, side to side, forcing the machine into various countermaneuvers and taking special note of the strategies it employed most often.

When I get close and threaten to barrel roll to the left, it nudges over aggressively. When I roll the other way, it seems to hesitate. Remember that.

"Tricky air-to-ground is coming up," Dex reported. "The touchdown needs to be steep, and there's a sharp turn in the road right away, so be ready to land hard and drift."

"Thanks," Mace said, clenching his jaw. He remembered flagging this very technical morph when he'd studied the route on his way back from Antarctica this morning, but unlike the rest of the drivers, he'd never had a chance to practice it. *No time like the present*, he thought, and he sacrificed a small amount of speed to make sure it went right.

It went better than right. *Academy* had a rough time with the transition, and Mace pounced. Abandoning his caution, he immediately stomped on the gas upon nailing the landing, and he drifted hard, nosing around the outside of *Academy*'s path. The back tires went off the road and peeled dirt, but when they caught asphalt, he shot forward and took the lead.

First place was a nice place to be, and he had no intention of ever giving it up. Problem was, he was drawing near to another pit stop.

He pulled in, where he was met by Juan Pablo and his cousin, Raul. Mace popped the canopy. It was cold outside, but the weather was clear. The rush of frigid air felt good.

He shot the cousins a thumbs-up. "Thanks for joining the crew on such short notice. I knew we could count on you guys."

"That call came in from the princess, and we were all

over it!" said JP. "First place! Keep it up!" he told Mace, handing him a water bottle while Raul and the rest of the pit team fueled and changed out tires and transformer modules.

I'd Like to Thank the Academy pulled into its designated slot. None of Hightower's crew approached the cockpit as they worked. Mace figured the actor was watching reruns of his talk show appearances and didn't want to be bothered.

Mace needed a breather, though. He opened his visor and downed his water, wetting his face, and manually loosened his smart seating to adjust his position and move around a little. He was more stiff and sore than he'd realized. Not a good sign.

One of the members of Caballero's pit crew noticed who was behind the wheel. "That's Mace Blazer," he said to the guy next to him. "What's going on?"

"Oh, that's not good," Mace mumbled. It had been a year since he'd last raced as a cryptic. He'd forgotten how careful he needed to be about showing his face.

"Go, go, go!" JP shouted, slamming down the canopy glass.

No time to worry about it now, he thought, flipping his visor back down.

Mace zipped away just as Aya pulled in, and he was on the road before *Academy* was done fueling. He had built a lead, but he knew it would be short-lived unless he found a way to relax and ignore the pain creeping into his arms and side.

"Dude!" Dex barked. "What did you do?"

"What're you talking about?"

"Broadcasters are going insane talking about *you*."

"One of the crew guys saw me."

"Cameras saw you, too, idiot! I've got Gimbal buzzing my phone right now."

"Tell her hi for me," Mace said. "Come on. We've got a race to win."

And the marathon sprint settled into an intense rhythm, with the world's most beautiful backdrop of mountain islands and glaciered peaks showing the way. In and out of the water, onto and over the land, the race ebbed and flowed, Mace losing and regaining his lead as the morphs continued. He was right about winning this thing on the roads. *Academy*, as smooth and steady as it was, couldn't quite get the hang of potholes and snowdrifts and rough patches of asphalt. It would swerve where there was no need and plow over obstacles it should have avoided. But Mace remained tense. Was the AI bluffing, trying to lull him into a false sense of security? 'Nauts attempted to psych each other out constantly. The mind game was half the battle with a competition this long. It was certainly possible that *Academy* had been programmed to fake out other drivers. Mace reminded himself that he couldn't let his guard down or take anything for granted.

Aya darted into fourth place coming out of the final pit stop. Akshara Brahma ran a distant fifth. The battle for the checkered flag was on, and it was clear to everyone that it would be a contest of wills between the sport's newest versus youngest contenders: The Leading Man, Katana, and Renegade. Dex confirmed as much in Mace's ear. "The rest of the pack is being left behind. You two are racing like the world depends on it!"

"Don't look now," Mace quipped, "but it does!"

"Finish strong, Mace. You know the others won't hold anything back." He heard the words through a searing burst of pain radiating outward from the cramped scar tissue of his rib cage. He wondered if he'd ever be able to draw a full breath again.

They entered the last channel, beginning a short swim toward Punta Arenas. Behind Mace, Aya gained position through the water. As they neared the final water-to-air morph, Mace drew upon all his training and experience to quiet the sharp pain in his rattling elbow and bruised side. The extra burst of concentration worked. The discomfort numbed to a dull afterthought. Speed was all that mattered.

But *I'd Like to Thank the Academy* let loose with its end-game antics right then, catching Mace by surprise in spite of his determination to never let that happen. Hightower, as a dark, undefined hand-waving mass, streaked past him in the shallow water, stealing the lead as *Academy* shot airborne in a risky but legal early morph.

Mace rose, punched out of the water, and turned into a plane for only a few beats. Ahead of him was the competition's final transition—the cliffs near where JP's nighttime duel had ended—and Mace knew it would be hard to retake *Academy* once the final stretch of road was underway. *Academy* was lightning fast inside the raceway, and the road that led into town was familiar country for the AI, as the site of most training runs over the past several weeks.

"Now or never," Mace grunted. He cut sharply upward

and rolled to the left, forcing *Academy* into a sharp counter-jab. But Mace had anticipated the AI's move. He was already rolling quickly to *Academy*'s weaker side and cut past the ghost vehicle right at the cliffs. Mace landed first, jostled violently to gain control of the road, and held steady for the ultimate sprint into the stadium, where one final lap would decide, quite possibly, the fate of the world.

Mace risked a glance at his rear display. Out of nowhere, *Untouchable* was coming in fast, hugging the shoulder, vying to overtake *Silverado*. Aya was immediately behind her, and she was gaining speed for a pass of her own.

Aya and Akshara went around Hightower at the same time. *Academy* didn't know what to do. It had never before experienced a close race with more than one opponent near the finish line! It veered one way, and then the other, but discovered it was locked into its current path and actually *slowed down* to let them by, as if surrendering the race out of sheer confusion.

Mace laughed but stopped immediately. His side was flaring in pain, but he also realized that Akshara and Aya weren't letting off, not one bit. They were coming in fast, and they both had Mace dead center in their sights.

The entrance to the raceway was rushing near. Mace realized his rivals were about to pull the same stunt on him, trapping him in a tight middle lane with no maneuverability. He had to hold them off! But cutting one way would leave the other driver free to pass on the opposite side.

He swerved back and forth, hoping for the best, but it didn't work.

Aya was the first one to see Mace's mistake. She darted in, forcing Mace to the outside lane. They came into the stadium side by side, with *Untouchable* veering toward the inside track, a hair's width behind Aya's bumper. *Academy* came up beside *Untouchable*, and all four racers were jammed in a tight square formation for the last lap of the Gauntlet Prix.

Locked to the outside lane, Mace was suddenly afraid *Academy* would calculate a safe third as better than nothing, tucking to the inside lane and denying Mace a shot at placing. He wasn't going to be able to shoulder in on the inside track. The decision was made for him. He'd have to go faster, for longer, on the outer lane to win the Prix.

And he had no safety equipment to protect him if things turned sideways.

Didn't matter. More lives than his own were on the line.

His foot pressed down on the gas pedal as if he could budge the Earth with the force of it.

They rounded the first corner, then the second, then the third, still holding steady to their respective positions. Mace had found the extra speed, but it wasn't enough for an outside pass this late.

The checkered flag was visible at the end of the next straightaway. Mace's side burst with pain. His elbow locked, and he cried out in agony.

"You okay, Mace?" Dex asked urgently.

"Not now," he barked back to his crew chief.

This is it. Find it. Find the speed!

But the finish line was gone.

The four contenders came around the bend, almost lapping *Paradox* and *Flipside,* who'd just entered the stadium.

They entered the pits still waiting on the final call from the line judge. The results appeared on screens throughout the raceway.

Mace was stunned into holding his breath. He had to read the boards several times before coming to grips with the story they told.

Katana had won the Prix. In a photo finish.

Mace had taken second, followed by only a few tenths of a second by Akshara Brahma.

The Leading Man, in fourth place, sitting in his front-row seat to all the action, wouldn't even make the podium.

CHAPTER TWENTY-SEVEN /////

The roar of the crowd in every direction was deafening. Mace leaned his head back in *Silverado*'s seat, finally feeling his muscles unclench and the stabbing pains piercing his arm and ribs. He drew a breath and caught it with a groan. The exhaustion and lack of sleep from the past several days consumed him. He closed his eyes.

"Second. Damn."

If I hadn't been so sore and rusty and sleep deprived . . . but he dismissed that. Such comments were for other people to point out, if they saw fit to. But even then, Mace would quickly admit that none of it mattered. It wasn't Aya's problem that he had been stupid in London. She was just as tired as he was, and she had piloted a *dicer* to victory.

"Good for her."

A knock at the canopy window snapped through his fatigue. Mace opened his eyes. "Need a hand?" Dex asked. Mace smiled and lifted the canopy. A few other members of the pit crew helped him to the ground. His team gathered around and congratulated him with as much enthusiasm as if he'd won.

"You might as well take off the helmet," Dex told him. "Everyone knows."

Mace chuckled morosely. He loosened his chinstrap and lifted the helmet off his head.

The crowd lost their minds.

Shouting churned and congealed out of the chaos into chanting. Mace heard one word over and over like a drum beat. "Renegade! Renegade! Renegade!"

On the grass in the middle of the raceway was a sea of media: cameras and boom mics stuck out as far as they could reach. Reporters from every corner of the globe were all screaming questions at once. Mace glimpsed Jax Anders pushing through the crowd. He was shouting something toward Mace about an exclusive interview. Mace gave him a thumbs-up and nodded. He waved brightly to everyone but otherwise ignored their shouting.

Over on the nearby dais, he eyed the first-, second-, and third-place pedestals with sudden anticipation. Then he noticed Thaddeus Hightower and Melanie Vanderhoof off to the side, gazing covetously at the Golden Gauntlet on a stand within a glass box. Melanie's expression was morose. Hightower was trying to look disinterested.

Nice acting, Mace thought. He laughed.

Rad Thad found Mace in the crowd and their eyes snagged on each other. Mace put a cuffed hand to his ear. *You hear that?* he mouthed, smiling brightly.

Hightower's expression soured. He averted his gaze and stormed away.

The path to the awards dais was always a slow crawl through enthusiastic crowds full of unfamiliar faces. Finally, all the milling 'nauts ducked underground for a breather. Mace was pleased to find Aya. The top two Gauntlet Prix placers broke from their swarms and met around the corner of a quiet hallway. Aya lifted her visor and huddled for a moment with Mace and Dex. "They're shouting your name. Totally friggin' typical." Aya's tone was bitter, but in a playful way.

"Everyone loves a comeback story. Congratulations, Aya," Mace told her. "In a *dicer*. That'll carry the day long after the excitement dies away."

Aya smiled warmly. "It was a close call all around. Could have broken a couple different ways."

"Hey, you pulled it off," said Dex. "Own it. I know I would."

"All three of you pulled it off," came a fourth voice.

It was Olesya. She was wearing a *Silverado* blazer and a Gauntlet Prix commemorative ball cap. Mace had forgotten that she was one of Dex's big sponsors.

"My dad isn't sure what to think about all this," she reported. "But he's promised me he'll break off the arrangement. I made him swear on it. He adores me, so I know I can make it stick."

"Have you seen Sentinel?" Mace asked her. "Someone has to catch him before he vanishes."

"He was in the skybox right until the end. Then he stormed off."

Linda Gimbal strode around the corner of the hallway

with a small cadre of associates.

"Drop your visor," Mace warned Aya. She flipped her iridescent glass down just in time to conceal her identity.

Linda Gimbal glowered at Mace, towering over him. "You better start explaining yourself."

"It's more complicated than you think."

"I have all day," she told him. "I award the Glove, and I'm not moving until I understand what the hell is going on."

"My crewmates here," Mace began, indicating Dex and Olesya. "They saved my life. They rescued me and Katana. They knew we were missing and put everything into finding us. They rescued us—from Antarctica."

Gimbal frowned in disbelief. "I heard you and *Lotus* were spotted coming in from the south. Is this true?" she asked Olesya and Dex. They nodded.

She turned back to Mace. "How long have you been racing as Caballero?"

"Only today. But I'm qualified for the Prix so I don't—"

"Quiet. That's not why I asked. Let me think. Why were you in Antarctica? None of this makes sense."

"Madam President, can we talk in private?" answered Dex.

She turned to Katana. "What about you? I need to know who you are. This is ridiculous."

"She was with me," Mace said. "You have no authority to make her reveal herself."

"Thanks for confirming she's a she," said Gimbal, "not that anyone ever really doubted that."

Mace looked at his feet. "I, uh . . . I meant that in a gender-neutral way," he tried.

"Knock it off, Blazer," Gimbal grumbled. She gave Katana and Dex a hard stare-down. Her eyes narrowed. "Let's duck into a locker room. We'll sort this out and then issue a joint media statement together."

She led Mace, Dex, Princess Vasko, and Katana into an empty room and plopped herself down heavily on a bench. "Start talking."

Mace explained everything that had happened over the past several days. He started with how he'd spied on Hightower, and how it had led him to being whisked away to Antarctica, to a top secret research and development facility. He revealed everything about Infinite Dynamic and Evander Sentinel and his fleet of AI machines. He included Sentinel's plan to win the Prix as a sort of grand Turing test triumph. And he ended with the harrowing escape involving outsmarting the robot fleet on snow and ice.

Gimbal remained quiet for a while before reacting. "Sentinel did come to me. He mentioned something about an exhibition of man versus machine. I sent him away immediately.

"I've tried to shut you down at every turn, Mace. I've made it my mission to ban youth from this sport. When you walked away on your own, I thought the problem was solved. Yet here we are. You always bounce back. You see what adults have been trained to ignore. If anyone was going to stop this kind of computer programming," she finished with a proud smile dawning on her face, and by scanning the room to consider Mace and all three of his friends, "it'd be the likes of you young people."

The room fell silent. Mace could hear the muffled footsteps and conversations of people scurrying about in the hallways. Linda Gimbal sighed. "Make your way to the dais. Let's wrap this up, and we'll figure out how to find Sentinel and bring him in. And congratulations, Ms. Nagata. You deserve this victory."

Gimbal left on her own. Aya collapsed back into the

lockers and took off her visor. "You hear that? She knows who I am. Now what?"

Mace scratched his head. "I'm not sure it's an issue."

Dex pulled them each to their feet. "Doesn't matter. There's no time. Let's get out there."

Aboveground, Mace was stopped before reaching the awards dais by a hand gripping his shoulder. "Enjoy the moment, Blazer. But you've done nothing to bring me down."

Mace turned and found Sentinel standing beside him. The tall, broad-shouldered man wore a suit and tie beneath a snow camo winter jacket. He wagged a familiar memory spike in one hand, teasing Mace.

"The Kreznians got scared. So, what? The line goes around the block."

"You don't think your other window shoppers are going to call you out after you took fourth place? Losing to three teenagers?"

Sentinel shrugged. "First place is a cryptic. Unfortunate, don't you think? I know who Katana is. But the public doesn't. Other buyers don't know how young the winner is. And the second it's revealed, the league will boot her. Right?"

Just then, a gang of Chilean soldiers marched forward.

They surrounded Sentinel, arriving from the direction of Linda Gimbal, who was over at the dais pointing at them as she talked to other officials. "You're coming with us. Don't make a scene."

But Sentinel smiled gleefully at them. He pocketed the memory spike and retrieved a laminated card. "You'll do nothing to me," he told the soldiers. "I have diplomatic credentials here from your president. You'll see that it kindly instructs you to leave me the hell alone."

The soldiers passed the card around, inspecting it. They nodded in agreement, reluctantly at first, but they handed the card back to Sentinel with total resignation. "Very sorry, Commander. You'll forgive us."

"No harm, no foul." Sentinel smiled, repocketing the card in his jacket.

"What?" shouted Dex. "No! Arrest him!"

"We can't," the lead soldier said.

"Take his memory spike! It has all the evidence you need!" Dex was turning red.

"We have no authority to do anything to this gentleman. He has immunity." The group of uniformed Chileans turned about-face and departed.

Mace's hands were balled into fists. He glowered at Sentinel. "I'll stop you myself if I have to."

"I've got a diplomatic free pass like this in most countries. You'll never stop me."

"Places, everyone!" shouted a stage director. "Ceremony goes live on my mark!" The TURBOWORLD camera crew and all the other media outfits from around the globe scrambled into position.

Sentinel shot Mace a final glare and walked away before Mace could say anything more to him.

"What was that about?" Gimbal asked Mace as they shook hands for the cameras.

"They let him go," Mace growled. "He has diplomatic immunity or something. Is that even a thing?"

Gimbal was surprised by this. "The Association has independent authority to conduct security operations as it sees fit," she pointed out. "But I don't have security units to apprehend someone like Sentinel. That's why I tried the Chileans. I'm not sure what's next, Mace. It might be out of our hands. Let's finish this ceremony and then we'll see."

Defeated and out of ideas, Mace shook his head but headed for the dais.

The Glove ceremony commenced.

In spite of Sentinel's escape and the soreness in his body—and in spite of his nagging disappointment in his second-place finish—Mace savored the moment when he and Aya mounted the dais together. Her opaque, iridescent helmet seemed to glow with pride at this finish to her hard-fought season. They both shook hands with Akshara Brahma, whose own satisfaction at coming in third was genuine but appropriately muted.

"I have to admit," Aya declared with a muffled voice. "This feels pretty good, being up here."

"I wish I could say the same," Mace grumbled. He watched Sentinel making his way out through the back of the crowd.

Linda Gimbal approached with the silver and bronze pins and the Prix Glove, sliding the latter onto Aya's outstretched hand.

Katana raised her gloved fist into the air. The crowds cheered her name. Mace eyed the elegant trophy longingly.

She had earned it. She'd been the best. Mace was proud of her even as he clenched his own fist in the knowledge that he'd wanted it for himself. *It's going to be okay,* he reminded himself. *There's always next year.*

He suddenly couldn't keep still.

"Take off your helmet, Katana," Gimbal instructed.

All three placers studied her cautiously.

"Do it." Mace winked. "You'll be glad you did. It's time the world knows what you're made of."

Hesitantly, she lifted her helmet, revealing her shining eyes and straight black hair.

Mace was looking for it, so he caught Sentinel's expression as the commander, standing unobtrusively in the crowd several paces away from the golden *I'd Like to Thank the Academy*, made sense of what he was seeing. Youths, all three of them: Aya and Mace and Akshara. Katana was just as young as Renegade. The announcement couldn't have come in a more humiliating way for Sentinel.

Turing test failed, he mouthed to the commander. Sentinel spun angrily and shoved his way farther back toward the golden racer.

The TURBO Association president spoke to the gathered crowd. "There used to be an indigenous tribe in these parts," she began. "The Yámana. A fascinating people, they were. As cold as it gets down here, they never used clothes. They stayed warm in other ways. They would sleep squatting, to preserve heat. They constantly applied seal blubber all over their skin as a protective layer. And they had a deep respect for fire."

Mace was only half listening. His eyes were like a hawk's, glued to a scurrying rodent. Sentinel popped the canopy of *Academy*.

You'll never stop me.

Mace battled back fury at the idea of him getting away. Just like Tempest Hollande. These rich people and their get-out-of-jail-free cards.

Gimbal was still delivering her remarks. "The Yámana never stayed in one place long. They were hunters and gatherers. The women would dive for shellfish, and that's mostly how they ate. When one beach ran out of food, the family would pack up and head out on a canoe to find another shore. They'd leave behind the homes they made, for the next family to use when the shellfish repopulated."

Academy's canopy lowered. Mace could hear the engine ignite. He fidgeted on his perch as he watched the golden morpher begin to crawl onto the open track.

"The amazing thing, though, is they took their fire with

them. As you can imagine, fire wasn't easy to produce in those days. They'd transfer their fire into their canoe and bring it with them to their next home. They never let their fire go out. The first European explorers who traveled through these lands would pass these very channels and see fires on almost every beach. That's one reason this part of the world is called the Tierra del Fuego. The land of fire."

I'd Like to Thank the Academy and Commander Sentinel were departing the stadium. No one was following them.

Gimbal turned to the podium, looking Aya and Mace and Akshara full in the eyes while she continued to speak to the crowd and to the world. "These young racers have conquered the odds. They have bounced back from defeat and overcome daunting obstacles. They carry their fire with them. Sometimes they carry it together, sometimes alone—but they always carry their fire. And that is why I am announcing here today that both Mace Blazer and Aya Nagata will be welcome back to race next year. And if I've learned anything about anything, they'll be joined by others just as young—and full of fire."

Stunned, the gathered audience initiated light, polite applause. But as the TURBO president's words slowly sank in, the volume of the crowd lifted and became a roar. Aya's excitement was plain to see. Mace offered her a congratulatory nod. She reached over and shared a long embrace with Akshara Brahama, who also seemed genuinely thrilled.

But Mace couldn't keep his eyes off the exiting trimorpher now a half mile down the track.

Aya turned to Mace, stooping for a hug. His embrace was hurried. "Aya . . ."

"What is it?" she asked.

"I . . . have to go. I'm going after him. Get ahold of JP. Tell him I need his uncle."

Aya followed Mace's gaze, and they both watched the distant *Academy* duck out of the stadium. "Go, Mace," she told him. "Do it."

Mace leaped from the podium and down off the dais in two giant bounds, to the delight of the crowds. He shouldered through elated fans, ignoring their outstretched arms, papers and pens, and requests for selfies, sprinting for *Silverado* parked off the track nearby.

///// CHAPTER TWENTY-EIGHT

The Tierra del Fuego mountain chain stretched off to the horizon, jagged and draped in snow. Endless icy glaciers gouged ruts down the forested mountainsides, emptying as waterfalls and streams and rivers into the network of ocean channels separating land masses. In the air, a golden fleck in the distance swayed to and fro, hugging the valleys and narrow lakes to duck radar detection. But *Academy* was not slipping away alone; Mace's eagle eye was locked firmly on his prey.

As Mace crept nearer, airborne, he stayed low to the

ground himself. He had no idea what his game plan was. All he could think to do for now was to maintain a visual.

Sentinel didn't seem to be aware that he was being followed. Mace wouldn't be drawing closer after such a late start, otherwise. Hopefully, he could continue inching up on—

Suddenly, those hopes were dashed. *Academy* morphed into a sub and darted underwater in a clear attempt to lose its tail. Mace knew this channel, though. It wasn't very deep. Instead of taking the bait, he rose higher and pushed the throttle harder, closing the remaining gap against the slower submersible and taking advantage of his overhead view over the waterway. *Academy* was clearly detectible as a dark shadow, and Mace had no trouble keeping tabs on its wake.

It wasn't long before Sentinel or *Academy* realized their mistake—a submersed morpher would never outrun a rival in the open air. The golden morpher came straight up out of the water like a rocket. Mace had to bank sharply to miss colliding with it. He craned his neck in an effort to relocate his prey. Finally, he spotted *Academy* arching up and over the next snowy mountain ridge. Mace rose against heavy g-forces to resume his pursuit.

No more prowling. The chase was on.

Mace could match *Academy*'s speed, but now that they were both engaged in a full sprint, he wasn't finding the extra juice necessary to overtake his adversary. The fleeing morpher was doing everything by the book—perfectly. Mace was certain the AI was in control at this point. Mace had to marvel: *Academy* was at the top of its game. It didn't know it had just lost the Prix; it harbored no regrets. How could it? It was simply a machine. A computer program, doing what it was designed to do: stay in the lead and cross the finish line first. And it was good at its job. *Academy* was incredibly difficult to catch, especially one-on-one.

Which made the thought of it learning to be a soldier horrifying. No emotion, no remorse, no conscience. Each step based on efficiency and speed. Maximizing carnage and death. . . .

An instinct pinged the back of Mace's brain. A new uneasiness. He dared a glance at his fuel gauge. It was low, the indicator light so red it looked crimson. Of course, it would be—no one ends a race on a full tank! No one had bothered to fuel her back up yet.

But *Academy* must be fully refueled. She was pointed

directly south toward the Drake Passage fueling station. Sentinel wouldn't have taken off without doing that.

I can't wear it out, Mace realized. *I have to take it down. Now.*

Uncertainty gnawed at him. Yes, he'd beaten *Academy* in the Prix, but that had involved playing the long game. He'd had hours to adjust to every inch of movement. And in Antarctica, he'd carried the high card, playing to Sentinel's low fuel. But how could he come out on top now, in the few precious minutes left to him, against *Academy*'s precision?

It was that word that stopped him short. *Precision.* It was a word based on a certain set of *rules*. But this wasn't a race—this was a hunt.

And in a hunt, there are no rules.

Mace laughed out loud. No checkpoints, no referees, no line to cross. *I don't need to beat him. I just need to stop him.*

But . . . *Silverado* was still gutted of safety equipment. *If I mess up, I could die!*

It was a strange realization. After all the pomp and circumstance of TURBO—the fans, the interviews, the flashbulbs, the commercials—even the surreal moment when Melanie had encouraged him to introduce himself to the

Sphinx—Mace Blazer suddenly felt like himself, with no audience watching, in this moment of real consequence.

His eyes narrowed. *Academy* had no clue what was coming. *I can use that.*

He crested and banked over the Tierra del Fuego mountaintops, framed by the deep blue of the unbroken sky. Mace hugged the contours of their snow-patchy black rocks, which suddenly fell away below him, widening into a gentler slope broken by trees. *Now or never.* He laid on the throttle, no holds barred, no regrets, aiming straight. *Take her out of the sky. Whatever it costs.*

The AI, true to form, treated his approach like it would in a race. It whipped sideways, blocking him out in a classic maneuver to deny him access to *Academy*'s wake. But the AI had never gone up against an opponent with no interest in passing it. *Academy* itself was Mace's target.

Stay in your lane.

For once I agree.

He pressed forward, closer, nosing straight behind *Academy*. A detached part of his brain registered that *Silverado* had started to glow red, like a space shuttle re-entering the atmosphere. But Mace didn't let up. He nudged forward and pushed the wheel hard. The two trimorphers collided, and both spiraled out of control.

His hand, trained to act automatically, fought the g-forces pinning him down. It found the ejector lever. He was airborne, watching a snowy ridgeline spin from somewhere . . . outside. His body was enwrapped in his smart cushioning, tumbling high over the jagged peaks. *Silverado*, releasing a contrail of black smoke, missed one outcropping, and pierced the next mountaintop. She exploded, littering the mountainside with debris. Mace could feel the blast of heat.

That's what I call a checkered flag.

Academy hit the snow at a better angle and skipped like a rock on water, finally tumbling and coming to a halt.

Mace's parachute billowed open. He figured out which way was down and stole a look: the ground was coming fast. He braced his legs for impact as he slammed into deep snow.

Mace freed himself from the smart cushioning. He rose on unsteady legs, suddenly deeply aware of his exhaustion. He pressed himself forward, trudging toward the wreckage of *Academy*.

At last, through a carpet of snow, he reached the trimorpher. He pressed the door-open button, and Sentinel slid out through the widening opening, falling heavily to the snow.

Blood caked Sentinel's mouth and chin. One leg jutted out at a strange angle, clearly broken. But he was breathing. He'd survived.

"Well, I guess we wait here," Mace said. "You okay?"

Sentinel spat blood at him but missed.

Mace's smile betrayed an odd, detached amusement at their current predicament. "So, should we make a pact? Give each other permission to eat the other one, if one of us dies first?"

Sentinel stared at him, exhausted and disgusted. When he finally replied, his tone was beaten: "What's wrong with you, boy?"

"Nothing," Mace said. The lightness in his heart made him want to laugh. "Not anymore."

"You know, we just might die up here. And for what?"

Mace's laughter bubbled to the surface. "For the sake of stopping you! That's what."

It wasn't too long—maybe half an hour—before the

sound of rotors penetrated Mace's ears. As he craned his neck to scope it out, a helicopter suddenly burst over the mountain peaks behind him. He waved, but the helicopter was already descending rapidly, zeroing in on the *Academy* crash site. Aya leaned out the window, hovering a few feet above the snow. Mace cracked a grin, which widened when he saw both JP and Chief Garcia pressing against the helicopter's back windows.

Chief Garcia tossed Mace a pair of handcuffs, and Aya prudently remained aloft until he'd locked them around Sentinel's wrists.

She landed the chopper a short distance away. She and the Garcias and Dex filed out of the cabin and made their way over.

"Sorry I blew up your trimorpher," Mace told Dex.

"I don't take it personally." He sighed. "You do seem to enjoy smashing up other people's rides."

"I don't suppose my fancy immunity card will impress you much?" Sentinel asked Chief Garcia as the Punta Arenas police chief lifted him onto his good leg.

Garcia shook his head as he began searching through the

commander's numerous jacket pockets. "I don't suppose it will. What's this we have here?" The police chief lifted the memory spike into view.

"You can't take that!" Sentinel struggled to free himself and fell back in the snow. He cried out and then lay still with a weak whimper of pain.

Garcia sighed. "Where should we keep him? My jail-house?"

Dex shook his head. "Actually, the TURBO Association has authority to oversee its own security, since it operates in so many different countries. I bet Gimbal will take custody of him until the Pentagon people get here and see what's on that spike."

"Great idea." Mace looked at Sentinel as he spoke. "They're not going to like your go-it-alone approach to government contracting, are they?"

"Get me off the snow, damn it! Before I freeze," Sentinel complained. He said nothing more.

Mace and the others helped him onto the waiting helicopter and secured him inside. Mace took shotgun next to Aya, and they lifted off.

"What did you do?" Aya asked him. "Can't leave you unsupervised for a minute."

"I smashed into him," Mace explained. "It was the only way."

She considered him silently for several beats. "You okay?" she asked.

"I am," he said, after thinking about it. "I really am."

ACKNOWLEDGMENTS

As with all books, this novel went through several drafts, and shed many pounds along the way. I'm forever grateful to the crew who helped make each draft race along smoother and faster than the previous. To my crew chiefs, David and Pete: thank you for all the hard work. And to the rest of the team: Camille, John, Alli, and Paul: this tale wouldn't have lifted off without your extensive input. Thank you.

I owe my mother, Bonnie, a special debt of gratitude for her role in getting me out there to explore the world. Mace's travels wouldn't be half as exotic or rendered with so much detail and affection without her guiding, adventurous spirit throughout the years.

And to my family, Clare, Ariel, and Everest: You're my audience of three. I write for you.

Any mistakes or inaccuracies, both intentional or accidental, are mine alone.